Welcome to The Oyster Bar

a story of love & death

BETH SORENSEN

This novel is dedicated to Reedville, Virginia:

My birthplace,

childhood summer home,

and the inspiration for Jett's Landing, Virginia.

The people and the land have shaped me into the writer I am today.

A Note From The Author:

Content Warning

Some readers may find the themes in my novels, including *Welcome to The Oyster Bar: a story of love & death*, disturbing. If you are sensitive to certain topics, please take a moment to read the content warning page on my website at www.bethsoren.com.

Chapter One

Tula

"Jesus, Tulip. It's a short flight from Key West to Richmond. Once you land, you can rent a car, or one of your sisters can pick you up." Frustration punctuated my father's voice. "I was a colonel in the United States Air Force. Get on the damned plane!"

I was the youngest daughter of one of the most decorated United States Air Force colonels ever to serve but was terrified of flying. Go figure.

"If God had meant for us to fly, we'd have been born with hollow bones and feathers," I said as I put the last items into my suitcase.

I don't know why my dad was arguing with me. We had been round and round on the topic twice before during the phone call.

I grabbed my moisturizer from the dresser to add to my bag and saw a photo taken a decade earlier that I kept wedged in the mirror's frame. It was of Dawson and me, hugging and smiling at a friend's wedding on the beach at the Outer Banks of North Carolina. Dawson was more like a brother than a cousin and was closer to my age than any of my sisters. If I had to give him one title, it would be that of best friend.

I can't believe he's dead.

The heavy feeling following the initial shock felt like it would be with me forever. I remembered feeling the same way when my mother died. My stomach soured at the thought.

I was going back to Jett's Landing for the first time since my mother's funeral to attend his. A tear escaped and slid down my face, and I quickly wiped it away. I didn't like showing emotion that way. I shoved down my sadness but knew it would bubble up again because it wasn't the first time I cried since hearing the news.

My dad, still on the other end of the phone, sighed. He knew this argument was pointless. We were both aware that, as his youngest child, his little princess, I was the most stubborn of all my siblings.

"Anyway, I don't think George would fly well, and I'm bringing him with me."

George heard his name and strolled into the room, dropping his furry golden retriever body at my feet. I leaned over, scratched him behind the ear, and remembered I needed to pack for him. A leash, food, treats, bowls, a brush, and toys were all it took to keep my five-year-old pup happy.

I closed my suitcase and carried it to the door before walking through the house one last time as I collected George's necessities and deposited them into a tote bag. To say I was still functioning on autopilot was an understatement.

When my dad called to tell me my cousin, Dawson DeWitt, had been murdered, so many questions flooded my mind. How did it happen? Was there a suspect? Why would someone do this? The more questions I asked, the angrier I became, especially since my dad knew nothing. I would have to wait until I got to Jett's Landing to hunt down the answers.

I immediately made a list of everything that needed to be done before heading to Virginia the next day. When I was finished writing it, I sat on the edge of my bed, giving myself a chance to sob while I was alone. If there were no witnesses, it didn't happen, and no one could claim to have seen the tears.

Luckily, my list was short. Mostly because of my roommate, Callie. While she rented a room from me in my Key West home, she was more than a boarder. She was my best friend in Florida. I could count on Callie to get the mail and newspaper, water my plants, and keep an eye on things.

After rolling out of bed the morning before I left and discovering what happened to Dawson, Callie immediately asked for my list. She knew me well. After she read it, she hugged me and said in her sleepy morning voice, "Call your boss at the newspaper, and I'll handle everything else while you pack."

She was still asleep the next morning when I glanced out my bedroom window, noting the brightening sky as daybreak approached. I loaded a few final things into the Jeep and found it was already hot and humid.

"The sun is finally up, so George and I are leaving now. I'll stop in Savannah tonight and be there sometime late tomorrow. Sorry, Daddy, it's the best I can do."

I knew when I called him "Daddy," it softened his frustrations. And the thing about me that frustrated him the most was my fear of flying.

Chapter Two

Tula

IT HAD BEEN A long two days of driving, but I knew I was only a few miles away from my final destination. We crossed the last of the six bridges it took to get there after getting off of I-95. The soft top was down on my five-year-old forest-green Jeep, and the humidity was high enough to form beads of sweat on the back of my neck, even though I was driving sixty miles an hour and the sun had set an hour earlier.

"George, you must be in dog heaven. All the joys of sticking your head out the window without having to even sit up." George woofed at me, and I smiled, patting him on the head. "I know. I'm tired, too, but we're almost there. Aunt Cookie will be thrilled to see you. Try to stay out of Uncle Parker's way. Don't take it personally. He doesn't like dogs in general. It has nothing to do with you."

It had been over a year since I had seen my dad, whom I was looking forward to spending time with, and could not remember the last time all four of my sisters and I were in one place at the same time. That was something I was not looking forward to. As I thought about my sisters and their lectures about me being single, childless, and rapidly approaching thirty, the cemetery and Methodist church came into view on the left.

I resisted the urge to pull onto Cemetery Road and stop. The family plot was full of people I loved, but there would be time for visiting the dead later. The living were waiting and anxious to see me.

I slowed down as I reached the fishing village's city limits. I still was not certain that Jett's Landing, Virginia, qualified as a city, but one thing was clear, it had not changed over the last decade. I drove past the cemetery and the newer homes in town. The six homes were built in the 1940s, and the locals continued to call them the new homes. J.P. Kline's General Store and Grocery was long closed for the day, but the dim neon sign on the building still flickered.

I passed Creek Road and counted the houses on the left. When I got to the fifth driveway, I turned but not before glancing at the Fisher House across the street. It was my favorite house in town. A beautiful three-story brick Victorian home. I always had the desire to buy it, but the last time it was on the market, I had just bought my home in the Keys, and there was no way I could afford a second home and certainly didn't need one.

Before my Jeep came to a complete stop, relatives poured out of my aunt and uncle's house. First, my dad, then two of my sisters, and finally, more nieces and nephews than I could count. How could they all fit inside the tiny Cape Cod-style home in the first place?

George hopped out, not waiting for permission, and went off in search of a bush.

"Finally," Dad said, engulfing me in a hug.

Compared to me, he was a giant. As short as I was, almost everyone over the age of thirteen seemed giant to me. Dad was around six foot three, with muscular arms and legs. He didn't look nearly as old as he was, and it was only his white hair and a few wrinkles around his eyes that hinted at his true age.

"It's about time, little princess."

Chapter Three

Paul

"Hey, Paul, our new partner is out front," Glenn said as he walked into the kitchen.

I checked the cook's jambalaya and gave it the okay to serve. We weren't open to the public after the funeral, but guests for Dawson's reception needed to be fed. I looked at Glenn, who was smiling. Glenn may have been happy about our new partner, but I wasn't.

"You know, I'm pretty pissed at Dawson. What the hell was he thinking, leaving his share of the restaurant to some outsider? I don't care that she's his cousin. She doesn't even live here. How the hell is some two-bit journalist going to be of any help to us? We all agreed to be partners, active in operating the restaurant, and now we're gonna be a person short." I thought for a moment. The decision came fast, like always. "I think I need to talk to this chick. She needs to understand that this is no free ride." I headed toward the main seating area.

Glenn tried to stall me by yelling, "Paul, you should probably know something about her."

I was already out the kitchen door and didn't hear Glenn's footsteps behind me.

I scanned the room, knowing Dawson's cousin would be with his parents, Cookie and Parker, but I saw no woman with them.

Cookie was an attractive woman. Even in her late sixties, she usually gave off an air of youthful energy. Today, though, a heaviness filled her heart, and it showed through her eyes. Her blonde and white hair was pulled into a French twist, and her black dress looked as though she hadn't worn it since the eighties.

Parker, who was drunk as usual, stood beside a man in his mid-to-late seventies. The man's posture read military. Next to him stood a girl, her back facing me.

She could not be our new partner. Judging by her height of maybe five feet, and her tiny frame, I figured she was either thirteen or fourteen. I watched as Cookie pointed across the room to Glenn, then over to me. The girl turned in my direction, and I realized she was no girl but a petite woman. The curves that weren't initially visible from the back exposed themselves when she turned in my direction. She was wearing a sleeveless black dress that fit her body perfectly, and her long curly hair cascaded along her shoulders and halfway down her back. I had never seen a hair color like hers. It wasn't dark enough to be called auburn but not bright or orange enough to be ginger. It was somewhere in between and highlighted with streaks of strawberry blonde. Her flawless, sun-kissed skin created a beautiful glow on her heart-shaped face. If she was wearing any makeup, it was minimal, but I was never a good judge of that.

Damn, she is gorgeous.

My mind went straight to the gutter. As soon as I thought of all the things I wanted to do to her, I was disgusted with myself. My best friend had just been murdered, and I was standing there, thinking about screwing his cousin.

The woman watched as I approached the group, her face void of expression, but her eyes were amazing. Large, round, and olive-green with golden flecks. I was mesmerized by them, and they left me speechless.

"Paul," Cookie said when I reached the group, "you should meet Tula. Tula, this is Paul Reed. Paul, this is Tula Yates, my niece."

We shook hands. Her soft skin was warm, the heat radiating a wave through my body. I did not want to let go but released it when she loosened her grip. Then the man next to her shook my hand.

"John Yates. It's a pleasure to meet you."

Tula wrinkled her nose.

"Dad, who was the last person that called you John besides Mom and Cookie?" She turned to me. "Everyone calls him The Colonel."

"That's true, Tulip," The Colonel replied, then looked at me. "But I'm long retired now. So, either is fine."

"Air Force?" I asked, noticing he had called her by a different name than her aunt did.

"Yes. Forty-three years."

"Wow! Forty-three years. That's a lifetime. Thank you for your service."

He acknowledged my words with a smile and nod.

This tiny woman next to me stunned me into silence each time I looked into her eyes. I had planned on giving her a lecture when I walked over to her about what was expected of her, but no words would come out. All I could think of was pressing her luscious lips against mine. She was talking, but my brain was wandering. So, I grunted and walked away, hoping to find sanity in another part of the restaurant.

Once I put some distance between us, I wondered what she thought about everything that happened with Dawson. I wished I had listened to what she was saying.

Chapter Four

Tula

EVEN THOUGH IT WAS technically closed to the public, "The Oyster," as the locals called it, was packed. Much of the town's population was in the dining area, eating and mingling. I scanned the room, hoping to see a few familiar faces. As I did, I was certain many people in attendance could—and at least one probably did—murder Dawson.

"Here's the thing, Tulip," Uncle Parker said as we stood in the restaurant. "He left you his part of The Oyster."

"What? Why?"

"No one knows. He left his bank accounts and other investments to your Aunt Cookie and me, but his part of The Oyster, he was very specific about."

"So, I own a quarter of this place?" I said, looking around.

The Oyster Bar & Grill was neither a bar nor a grill. It had a small bar in it, but it was a restaurant. A nice restaurant. A great place for a date night, a family dinner, or a quick bite after spending a day out on the Chesapeake Bay.

The dining area was casual but had an upscale feel. The cherrywood tables and chairs were perfectly placed across the room, maximizing the use of the floor without packing them too tight. They were covered with crisp white tablecloths, and small oil-burning hurricane lanterns adorned the center of each one. There were few solid walls and floor-to-ceiling windows highlighted beautiful views of the Chesapeake Bay, Connelly's Creek, and The Stack.

The Stack was a historic brick smokestack from the original fish processing plant near Jett's Landing and was a landmark for the locals on both land and sea. For years, it sat, abandoned and crumbling, until a local group of business owners and residents gathered to save it, having it declared a historic landmark, and then fundraised heavily to cover the extensive repairs.

The last time I saw The Stack, it looked as though a strong breeze could topple the hundred-thirty-foot-tall structure. When I looked at it through the restaurant windows, it was covered in scaffolding. The restoration was nearly complete, and it looked beautiful. I heard that the project was slated to be completed before the Fourth of July.

My Aunt Cookie grabbed my attention and pointed. "That's one of the owners, Glenn."

Glenn was short and overweight. His clothes were wrinkled, and he held a disheveled appearance with his crooked tie loose on his neck. He looked neither strong nor smart, but there was a familiarity I could not pinpoint.

"I've seen that man before. I just don't know when or where."

"You've got a good memory. I'm sure it will come back to you."

I focused on his face, but nothing clicked.

"And there's another partner, Paul."

I turned in his direction and looked him over. I noticed him at the funeral. He was wearing a black suit, a gray dress shirt, and no tie. His dirty-blond hair blew around during the graveside service until it was a mess, but every hair was back in place. His beard was well-trimmed and displayed his strong chin and cheekbones. The look worked for him, but he wasn't my type.

No one was my type.

Paul was tall and broad-shouldered, with lagoon-blue eyes I did not notice until after the introductions were made. He was probably the tallest man I had ever met. In addition to his height, he was a solid mass of muscle. His biceps were the size of my thighs, and I may have stared at them a little longer than I should have. I wondered if he was the type who spent all of his time in the gym. If I stripped off his black Oyster Bar T-shirt, I was certain I would find chiseled six-pack abs. I knew the narcissism of some men who put lifting weights and buying more hair gel above everything else. I almost married one and did not want to have to deal with one ever again.

Why in hell am I thinking about this man's body?

There was a reason I didn't do relationships anymore, yet I was standing there, for the first time in years, undressing a man in my mind.

Snap out of it, Tula!

My aunt made introductions, and we shook hands. He was strangely quiet, but I was not exactly a talkative person that day, either. I was still in shock that Dawson was dead and left me his part of this establishment.

"Well, I guess I should meet with everyone this week to figure out how this is going to work. I mean, I live in Key West. I can't be there and in Virginia at the same time." Paul growled quietly, turned, and walked away.

I looked at Cookie. "Is he always like that?"

"Yep," a baritone voice said from behind me. I turned to see the man who had been pointed out to me at the funeral as the third partner, Steven Faulkner. "You must be Tula."

I turned toward him and nodded as we shook hands. "And you're Steven, right?"

"The one and only," a waitress said as she walked up behind him. "He's a legend in his own mind." A beautiful woman with long bleached blonde hair smirked as she balanced a tray full of steaming hot shrimp and continued toward the buffet table next to the bar.

"That's Shawncy, my little sister. She waits tables when the bar is staffed and we need help on the floor. She's our bar manager, but she's great about helping wherever we need her."

"Who called out tonight?" Cookie asked.

"Jenny. She came in for a while, wanting to help with the wake, but it was too upsetting for her. She couldn't do it. They hadn't been together very long, but I don't know if she'll ever bounce back enough to come back to work here." He turned his attention to me. "I'd like to talk to you if you have a second."

I knew that name. Dawson dated a girl named Jenny about three months prior to his death. I could only assume by the comment Steven made that it was the same woman.

"Okay." He motioned down a hallway, and I followed him. We walked through the door at the end of the hall, and Steven closed the door behind me.

I took a moment to examine him. He was about six feet tall, lean, with dark-brown hair, brown eyes, and a faint scar across his forehead.

Steven pulled out an old office chair in front of an industrial-looking metal desk. When he did, I noticed a wedding band on his left ring finger. I shook my head and opted to stand. On the bulletin board behind him was a schedule pinned to it. At a glance, I saw that Dawson was scheduled to work Thursday. I would have to figure out what to do before then.

"Look." I knew when a man started a sentence with the word *look*, it meant one of two things. Either he was lying, or he wanted something. Steven moved until he was within inches of me. His body language screamed desire, but it did not work on me. "I'm gonna just get to the point." He wrapped one arm around my waist, pulling my hips toward his, and I looked up at him. "I want you to sell your part of the restaurant to me. I have big plans for this property."

What the hell?!

Everything was wrong with this whole scene. I peeled his arm away from me and stepped back. I didn't know what Steven's plans were for the restaurant, but Dawson entrusted me with his life's work, and I needed to do the right thing. As for his advances, they were creepy and he was married.

"Steven, I don't know what you were just thinking, but if you ever—and I mean ever—try that on me again, you'll be icing your balls down for two days. As for The Oyster, I'm sure you and the guys are worried about me bulldozing in and trying to change things. That's not my plan. I don't want to make any rash decisions, either. So, for at least a few weeks, I'm holding onto my part. Just remember to keep your distance. And at my cousin's funeral reception, too? Disgusting."

I stormed out of the office. I hadn't decided on my plan yet, but his cavalier attitude and inappropriate behavior made me more determined than ever to stay and get a feel for what was going on at The Oyster Bar.

While the wake continued inside the restaurant, I sat on the screened-in deck and stared at Connelly's Creek and The Stack. The locals called the fish processing plant the "fish factory," which operated on the same property as The Stack since it was built in the early 1900s. It was the only reason Jett's Landing prospered. It employed a large percentage of the town, and many families passed the skills needed from one generation to the next.

As I stared across the water, I considered Dawson's partners. Something in my gut told me one of them murdered Dawson. I was certain I'd seen Glenn before, and Steven was a creep. While I vaguely remember the two from my childhood, it had been so many years that I couldn't have picked them out of a crowd. I had never met Paul before the wake. Dawson spoke highly of him, but all I knew was what he told me about him.

I shook the thought from my head. I wondered if I was turning this into a suspense novel in my mind. A girl inherits part of a restaurant from a murdered relative, only to discover three mysterious partners who could have killed him for reasons yet to be revealed.

Yep, my reality sounded like a *New York Times* best-selling novel.

Chapter Five

Tula

I STRETCHED OUT ON DAWSON'S bed, staring at the ceiling as a bead of sweat rolled down my temple. Cookie and Parker had air conditioning in their home, but Dawson's room was partially above the kitchen and dining room, with west-facing windows next to the bed. It was like a sauna but provided privacy I couldn't get elsewhere in the house.

What the hell was Dawson thinking?

I knew The Oyster was his whole world, but he knew it was not a world in which I wanted to live. Dawson did a lot of the food prep, and I was no chef. I made a decent pie, and people liked my cakes and cupcakes, too, but this place wasn't a bakery. It was a restaurant with a small yet proper bar. I knew less than zero about how a restaurant functioned.

I should have gotten in my Jeep with George and headed home to Key West earlier in the day when my dad and sisters left. However, I was enjoying my time in Jett's Landing. Regardless of the fact that I went back for a funeral.

After lying there for a couple of hours, contemplating everything, I decided to stay a few more days. The guys were going to need help at The Oyster until they could get someone in to do Dawson's job, and the experience might make a good article for my column back home. Even as I formed the plan, I knew it would not pan out that way. I would be in Virginia for more than a few days. I would probably be there for a while.

I picked up the phone and dialed Callie. She answered on the third ring.

"Hey, Tula. How's it going?"

"Okay. The funeral was fine, I guess."

I was trying to sound nonchalant and thought I was succeeding until Callie spoke.

"I know that tone. What's happened?"

"Dawson left me his part of The Oyster Bar & Grill."

"So, now you own part of a bar? I swear, every good thing just falls into your lap."

Callie had no idea how far that statement was from the truth. She knew about my family and my day-to-day life in Florida, but I kept parts of my past hidden from her. I kept it from everyone who didn't already know about it.

"It's more of a restaurant, really. But what all of this means is that I'm going to need to stay up here a week or two longer than I had planned. I hate to do this to you, but can you keep taking care of things there?"

"Sure. You got a couple of envelopes in the mail that aren't bills or junk. Do you want me to send them to you?"

"No, I should be home by the Fourth of July. I'll take a look then."

"Sounds good. I'll put them on your desk. Have you met the other partners? What are they like?"

"Yeah, I met them at Dawson's wake. All men."

"You know, a wake is supposed to happen before the funeral. Not after."

"Don't blame me. I didn't name it or plan it. The guys did a good job of putting it together, though."

"Maybe Mr. Right is one of those partners."

"Callie, there is no such thing as Mr. Right. It's an urban myth. Like alligators in the New York City sewers. And at least one of them is married. But he's a creep. He tried to make a move on me at the wake."

"Gross. So, none of them were attractive?"

"I didn't say that. There was one that—"

"You know, even a one-night stand would do you a lot of good."

"Not my scene. You know that. Anyway, you should never sleep with business partners."

"Says who?"

"Says me!" I replied. "There's one thing, though. One of the partners, Glenn, looks so familiar. I just can't seem to place him."

"I'm sure it will come to you."

We talked about concerns she had with the plumbing, and afterward, I wandered downstairs to make my way to the fridge for a bottle of water. The kitchen looked like something from a 1950s television show. White-painted wooden cabinets were wedged into a small room with a refrigerator tucked into a corner. A white Formica-and-chrome table stood against the wall with four chrome and blue padded chairs tucked into it.

When I entered the room, Cookie was sitting at the kitchen table, making a shopping list. As she wrote, tears dripped from her eyes onto the paper, smearing the ink.

"Aunt Cookie? Is there anything I can do to help?"

She looked at me and wiped her tears from her face.

My heart broke for her. I didn't need to ask why she was crying or what was wrong. Her son, her only child, had been murdered less than a week ago. Actually, I was surprised I had not seen more tears. However, she was so much like my mom, a pillar of strength. When Mom was dying of cancer, Aunt Cookie stayed with us and helped during her final days. She came, specifically, to care for me. Dad could fend for himself, even though he was hanging on by a thread, but I was still a teenager in high school and needed a fully functioning adult. My sisters were all grown and had flown from the nest years earlier, as I was eleven years younger than the next child. Mom and Aunt Cookie showed such grace in those final days. It was a strength and calmness I had learned from and drew upon on more occasions than I wished were necessary.

"No, honey," she replied. "Come sit with me. I imagine you'll be heading back soon."

"Actually, I wanted to talk to you about that. I think I'm going to stay in Jett's Landing a little longer. I want to get things squared away with Dawson's partners before I head home."

"Oh, that's wonderful. I love having you around." She managed a small smile.

"I'm enjoying being back in Jett's Landing."

"It hasn't changed much, has it?"

"The only things different since I was here last are the restaurant, one new shop, and the condition of The Stack. The last time I saw it, it was in really bad shape. It looks like it's going to be a beautiful landmark when they are done."

"The group of business owners that raised the money has done a fantastic job. Hopefully, these repairs will keep The Stack standing for a long time."

"I'm amazed it was still standing at all when they started fundraising. Any thoughts on where I could rent a room? I can't expect you to keep me here as a guest."

Pursing her lips, she peered at me, furrowing her brow. "You will not rent a room somewhere. You are staying right here."

"Aunt Cookie—"

"It's not up for discussion. We're family. You'll stay here." I liked the thought of staying, but I wasn't sure it was a smart idea. She sensed my hesitation. "What?"

"Uncle Parker hates George. I can't ask that of him."

"Parker only dislikes dogs when he's sober. So, it will be fine."

I sat, wondering if I was about to cross a line. "When did his drinking get so bad? I've always known he drank more than he should, but what I've seen during this visit is a whole different level."

"I know, honey." She always called me honey, just like Mom. They were so similar that you would have thought they had been raised together, but Cookie was my dad's half-sister. "It picked up a little when he retired and then again when he was recovering from his knee replacement. Last week, though, when Dawson left us, it skyrocketed. I don't know if it will ever come back down. Luckily, he's not a mean drunk. Never has been. But lately, he's been blacking out. I'm worried about him. Have been for years. I guess it's the pitfall of falling in love. You get the bad with the good, but you know that."

She was right. I knew that. I knew it all too well.

"Has he considered getting help?"

"Parker says it's too expensive and that he can quit anytime he wants."

I sighed, knowing well and good it was more serious than that. "I can help pay for rehab if you ever convince him to go."

"That's sweet, but we can afford it. It's just his excuse."

"Speaking of affording, if you are serious about me staying, I plan on paying rent."

"No, you will not! You are my niece. You stay as long as you want."

I was about to argue the point with her when the kitchen's wooden screen door slammed shut. It always did, no matter how quiet the person entering the house was trying to be.

It was Uncle Parker with a case of beer under each arm. George took the opportunity of the open door to go outside.

"So, the little princess is staying?" he asked, slurring his words as he smiled. "I guess that means the cute little furball is staying, too."

I never really minded my nickname, except when Uncle Parker used it. Coming out of his mouth, especially when drunk, sounded weird. Hearing anyone else but my father say it didn't sound right to me.

"Not for long, Uncle Parker," I said as I watched him put the beer on the counter. "And as long as it's okay with you. I just want to be sure things are set at The Oyster Bar before I head home."

"That's fine," he said patting me on the head.

I was short. I didn't need a constant reminder of it. I hated when he did that, and he knew it, but he did it anyway. I think he enjoyed it because it made him feel tall, although he was short in stature. I would not comment about it though because it would anger my uncle and that would upset my aunt. Like my mother, she was a peacemaker. If everyone was not happy, they weren't happy.

"I know it will help Cookie cope." Even drunk, he loved and cared about my aunt. I could only figure that was the reason she never left him. No matter how bad his drinking got. "Just be careful. I'm pretty sure one of Dawson's partners killed him."

"What makes you say that?"

"A lot of things. The big one is that I heard him arguing on the phone with one of the guys the night before he died. I think it was Paul. I even told the police that. But they don't listen."

He grabbed a couple of beers from one of the cases, put the rest of the box in the fridge, and headed to the living room to watch TV and begin his evening ritual of drinking and watching one of the twenty-four-hour news channels.

Chapter Six

Tula

I COULDN'T SLEEP, ALTHOUGH I felt exhausted. I lay in bed, with George at my feet, snoring. Looking out at the moon through the window beside the bed, which was tucked into a corner of the room, I thought about the last time I talked to Dawson. He seemed nervous and distracted from the moment I answered the phone.

"Dawson, what's eating at you?" I said as I dropped a piece of popcorn into my mouth.

When he called, I was in the middle of watching *Gone With The Wind* again. It was my favorite movie, but I didn't mind pausing it to talk to him.

Dawson was my touchstone. My only real connection to my family, outside of my dad. As an outsider, most people would have thought I suffered from some family trauma that caused me to distance myself from my family, but I chose this exile. I had set everyone apart about five years ago. No one appeared to take the decision personally, and for that, I was thankful.

"Nothing. How's the book coming?"

"You know, you're the only—and I mean the only—person who knows that I'm working on one. Dad doesn't even know. You tell, and I swear I'll kill you. And, to answer your question, the revisions are coming along, I guess." A long pause made me think we had been disconnected. "Hey, Earth to Dawson. Is anybody home?"

"Tula, something's about to happen. I'm pretty sure I'm going to go to jail for it, too."

It was only then I heard the fear in his voice, and it worried me.

"Then, don't do it."

"The damage is long done. It was done years ago. Trust me. I don't think I can stop this. I dropped a letter in the mail to you today. It explains everything."

"No, tell me what's going on now. You're scaring me. Do you need me to come up to Virginia?"

A door slammed in the background on Dawson's end. "Hey, I gotta go. I'll call you tomorrow. We'll talk more then."

He did not say goodbye.

He just ended the call.

And then Dawson was gone.

Within minutes, he was dead.

Chapter Seven

Tula

STEVEN AND PAUL LOOKED befuddled when I walked into the office at four on Thursday afternoon. The other partner, Glenn, was nowhere to be seen. We stared at one another for a moment before Paul finally said something.

"Hey, Tula. I don't mean to sound rude, but why are you here?"

He didn't sound rude. He sounded curious.

"Well, I noticed Dawson was on the schedule for tonight, and since his part of this place is now mine, I thought it right to show up. It comes with the following disclaimer, though. I know nothing about the restaurant business."

"Great, so, basically, you are no help to us," Steven murmured and rolled his eyes. "You're just going to be in the way."

Of course Steven would have an attitude.

"I figured you needed the help. Dawson gave me the impression it was a hands-on partnership. If you don't want me here, I'll leave. I'd rather be in Key West, anyway."

"Wait," Paul said, sounding thoughtful, "we'd have to train a new employee, anyway. We'll just train you. Come on, follow me."

This did not sound like the same brooding, silent Paul Reed I met a few days ago. He seemed kind and had a pleasant voice. As we walked down the hall toward the seating area, I needed to tell him a few things. However, the walking wall was moving so fast I was nearly jogging to keep up.

"Can you slow down? Short people have short legs."

Paul stopped and ran his fingers through his hair as he looked at me. "Sorry. I forget how tall I am sometimes. How tall are you, anyway?"

"My driver's license says five-foot-two."

"But . . ." He smiled, knowing it was not true.

Smirking, I shook my head. "Five feet, if I'm wearing shoes. And you?"

"You don't want to know." I nodded, and he continued. "Six-foot-four, barefoot."

I sighed.

We continued walking as Paul now seemed to be aware of the speed at which I moved and adjusted his pace to mine. He allowed me to get in front of him before we went through the kitchen door. When we did, I froze, and Paul ran into me. I stumbled forward, but he caught me by the waist to steady me. My untucked T-shirt pulled up when I stumbled, and his warm, strong hands were soft against my skin. I exhaled a jagged breath and looked down at his hands.

"Are you okay?" he asked as he slowly removed his hands from me. "I didn't mean to plow you over."

I looked around the kitchen again. It looked like uncontrolled chaos, and the restaurant was not even open yet.

"Holy Mother of God, help me."

"You've never been in a restaurant kitchen, have you?"

I shook my head.

What the hell did I agree to?

"Don't worry. It's not as crazy as it looks. Come on, let's teach you how to do something."

I spent the rest of the night wrapping clean silverware in fresh white cloth napkins and making sure the bathrooms were clean and stocked.

When I got back to my aunt and uncle's house at one in the morning, I fell into bed, fully clothed, and was asleep before my head hit the pillow.

Chapter Eight

Dawson's Killer

IT WAS AFTER TWO in the morning when I quietly opened the door and let myself into the house. I walked to the fireplace mantle and picked up one of the many framed photos. My wife stuck them there soon after we moved in.

In the moonlight shining through the window, I stared at the outline of two people. Two teenagers, Bella and me. She looked gorgeous. I didn't love her, but I loved her body. She had no idea I would end her's and several other people's lives. Then I would marry her sister. I let the sweet young girl fall in love with me while I consoled her loss. Unbeknownst to her, I had destroyed her family. Too much alcohol, too many drugs, a speed boat, and a cocky attitude were catalysts for what I had done that night.

It was the first time, but it wasn't the last.

The last was Dawson. The idiot couldn't keep his mouth shut. He was the first man I killed. It wasn't nearly as much fun as killing women. Still, I needed to protect myself from the consequences of those nights. Regardless of Dawson's promises to keep my secret, if I were exposed, it would be the end of my life, and I would never feel the adrenaline rush that I got from fucking and killing women again.

I couldn't think straight now that Tula was in town. My mind went into overdrive, thinking of all the perverse things I wanted to do to her tiny body. Her uncle, Parker DeWitt, would kick my ass if he knew what I thought the day I met her. If he didn't, Paul Reed would. I saw the way he looked at her. He was half in love with that woman the moment he set eyes on her.

I had to leave Jett's Landing soon. It wouldn't be hard. I knew exactly how to slip away. However, I needed to make one more person disappear first.

Chapter Nine

Tula

I HATED CHOPPING VEGETABLES for the sides, but it seemed like it was the only thing Paul would ever let me do in the kitchen, even after working twelve-hour days, six days a week for the last ten days. It was a magnificent kitchen. I could only dream of the things I could bake in it. The industrial stainless-steel workspaces were spacious and well-organized. I had watched enough reality television to know most restaurant kitchens were cramped. Multiple walk-in freezers and refrigerators lined the back wall with sinks against the wall to the right. The ovens and stovetops were better than anything I had ever used, not that Paul would ever give me the chance.

I went into one of the walk-in refrigerators and brought out a box of broccoli that was delivered that morning. There wasn't enough washed and prepped to get through the night's dinner rush. The Oyster Bar went through more broccoli and hollandaise sauce than anyone could imagine. Once I tasted it, I understood why.

The recipe had been in Glenn's family for a few generations. It was rich and velvety smooth, with the slightest hint of lemon against its buttery goodness. I'm certain I gained five pounds just looking at it, let alone eating it. However, it was worth every single calorie.

I set the box by the sink, washed each head, and then set it all on the prep counter. Paul was watching me out of the corner of his eye. He had only shown me how to do this once, and I was repeating everything exactly how he had done it. When I was done washing the broccoli, I retrieved the proper knife to silently complete the task.

I liked working in the kitchen. No one felt obligated to hold polite conversation or pass along gossip. However, if you wanted, you could find friendly conversation. Even among the chaos in prepping food for the dinner rush, it was peaceful.

I looked up just in time to see Paul turn his eyes away from me. Had he been staring at me? I felt like he had been doing that a lot lately.

Why doesn't he trust me to get the work done up to his standards?

I bit my bottom lip and thought about it. My focus was only lost for a split second before the cold blade of the knife sliced into my index finger. I pulled my hand back, and the knife clanged as it hit the tiled floor.

As soon as Paul heard the clank, he called out without looking up. "Whoever dropped that better pick it up fast. You know I get pissed when my knives end up on the floor."

"Damn it all!" I loudly cursed, wrapping my good hand around the bloody finger. I ran to the sink and blasted the cold water, shoving both hands under it.

Paul finally turned, saw the bloody water leaving my hand, and rushed over to me.

"Jesus, Tula, how bad is it?" he asked as he grabbed a clean towel from over the sink and put it out for me to lay my hand in.

"I don't know. I haven't looked."

"Let's take you back to the office and examine it. There's a first-aid kit there."

Chapter Ten

Paul

"REALLY, PAUL, I'LL be fine. I'm sure it's not that bad."

I turned off the water, and we watched as the cut bled again. I looked down at her. For a girl who had recently had a day off, she looked tired. It was obvious she wasn't sleeping, and I was certain it was the reason she lost focus and cut herself.

I wrapped her hand in the towel and led her back to the office. Steven was working on the quarterly taxes and stopped to investigate. She reluctantly plopped into a chair and unwrapped the towel. Tula had not severed the finger but would need stitches. Real stitches, not surgical glue.

"Dammit, Paul, I'm sorry." She let out a long sigh. "I guess I'm gonna have to drive myself to the hospital."

"Drive with your finger like that? You do know the closest hospital is thirty minutes from here?" Steven asked as he stood, looked at her hand, and headed for the door but not before looking at me. "Not only is she no help, but she's a problem now, too."

"Not true, asshole. She's more help than you are around here."

After I watched Steven leave the office, I looked at the clock, forming a plan. I hated the thought of her having to drive that far, and I couldn't afford to let someone from the restaurant drive her. Jenny was still taking a leave of absence, and two busboys called out. It was four forty-five. I had an idea if I could pull it off.

"Sit tight for a second." I pulled my cell phone from the pocket of my jeans, unconcerned that Tula's blood was on my hands, staining everything I touched. "Good afternoon, Maggie. It's Paul Reed. Is Dr. Floyd still there? Could I talk to him for a second? Sure, I'll hold." A moment later, I made a face that probably looked like I had eaten a sour grape. "Worst hold music ever. Here, listen to this." I put my phone on speaker, and vintage seventies disco converted into elevator music blared through the speaker. Tula, who rarely reacted to anything when I was around, laughed, and her response caught me off guard.

That is the best sound I have ever heard.

I smiled, listening to the soft, sweet tone of her voice until Dr. Floyd answered.

"Hey, Paul. How's it going?"

"Good, but I need a favor. My best kitchen help has sliced her finger open. If I run her up to your office, could you stitch her up?"

I was not lying. She was the best help I had in the kitchen. She never asked what to do or how to do it. Once she was trained, she had the assignment done to perfection. She would finish one thing, assess the state of the kitchen, and move on to something else. Silverware was always wrapped, the bathrooms stayed spotless, broccoli was always prepped, and the kitchen counters were always freshly wiped down.

"I can do you one better. My wife's out of town at a church retreat. Why don't I come stitch her up there and grab some dinner?"

"Sounds good. Dinner is on the house tonight, though," I said, grateful for the generous offer.

"Then, so are the stitches."

The doctor and I finished our conversation. After, I turned to Tula, whose vision and thoughts were somewhere far away.

"Penny for your thoughts?"

My voice snapped her out of her dazed state.

"You would think inflation would change that statement after being said for so many years."

It was obvious she was trying to avoid answering the question.

I inevitably laughed. "So, what would it be now? A dollar for your thoughts?"

"I was thinking a Hamilton for your thoughts, but I suppose a dollar would do."

I watched as the corners of her mouth turned upwards into a full-fledged smile. It was effervescent.

I shook my head, smiling to myself, before looking down at her injured finger. "After you get stitched up, I'm sending you home. You won't do me any good all bandaged up."

"We're already short-staffed. I'll stay and work the hostess stand. Get the hostess to wait tables or help in the kitchen. If I can't help you, at least I can greet the guests and seat them."

She was a hardworking woman. Tula had only been with us a short time, but she gave one hundred and ten percent to everything she did, and while I had not given her too many tasks to take on, she was a fast learner.

"Then, I'll go get you a clean Oyster Bar shirt. Yours has blood on it."

"Hey, Paul, I need a favor."

I was rising out of my chair when she started to speak but sat back down.

"Name it."

"You asked what I was thinking about?" She paused as though she were carefully choosing her words. "Can you make sure I'm never alone with Steven? He tried to make a move on me the first time we met. And I get weird vibes from him. I know it sounds stupid but—"

"No, if you don't feel comfortable with him, then you will never be alone with him."

"Thanks."

She didn't even know me, and she was entrusting her safety to me. Everything I felt for her settled into my soul. This woman could be my alpha and omega. My everything. I needed her to be mine.

I took a deep breath before continuing. "Honestly, he's not my favorite person either. He treats women like they're disposable. It's wrong. On top of that, he's married, and they have a baby. And now he wants to level the restaurant and sell the land to a developer."

"So, that's why he wanted to buy me out."

"Son of a bitch! When did he talk to you about that?"

"The first time I was here. At Dawson's wake."

"Damn, he wasted no time. I just don't understand why he wants to give this place up. I've offered to buy him out, but he wants more than his stake in the restaurant is worth, and this shady land developer is willing to pay."

"Paul, I don't wanna start drama. I really don't. I just don't trust him, and I don't feel safe around him."

"Thanks for coming to me and letting me know everything. I'll keep Steven away from you. As for the restaurant itself, I'm not selling The Oyster under any circumstances."

"I figured as much. I get the impression you love this place like Dawson did. Don't worry. I won't let Steven position himself so he can sell the place, either."

It was time for me to deal with that slimeball once and for all. I didn't want him to be a partner in the restaurant, but Dawson insisted on it. It was a deal-breaker for him, so I conceded.

I was going to kick Steven's ass. In the last two years, I had gotten complaints from waitresses—and one from a customer—about his inappropriate behavior. The man liked to flirt a little too much, was handsy, and had issues knowing when to stop. Messing with Tula was the last straw. This would end the next time we worked together. But at that moment, Tula needed all of my attention.

"I can see why you were Dawson's favorite cousin."

I, once again, noticed her bloodstained shirt, and as I stood, I saw the blood on mine as well. As I headed to retrieve clean T-shirts, Tula looked at me, and I was entranced by her eyes. Everything about her was amazing, but her eyes were magical. Each time I gazed into them I saw something new. That time, it was tiny specks of emerald within the olive just before it reached her onyx pupils.

Chapter Eleven

Tula

I RUSHED INTO THE OYSTER, twenty minutes late for work. I forgot to set an alarm and woke up five minutes before I was due to be at the restaurant. I dropped Paul a text to let him know before I raced to feed George and then jumped into the shower but never got a response.

I wasn't even through the door when I heard shouting coming from the office. The staff was scurrying around as they do just before opening. However, they were as silent as the dead and avoided doing anything that put them near the office.

"Fuck no! We're not selling the restaurant, and that's final!"

I never heard Paul angry before, but his booming, furious voice was not something I wanted to hear.

"You know, you might not get a choice. Glenn will side with me. We're both natives, not a couple of come-heres!"

Even though generations of my family had lived in Jett's Landing, I was still called a *come-here*, a term used for someone who had come to Jett's Landing to live. Not born and raised there. It was not a term of endearment.

As I listened to the argument, Barbi, the newest waitress, walked over to me. She was beautiful, with coffee-colored skin, waist-length braids, and large round eyes. They were an unusual color, nearly slate gray, and I wondered if she wore colored contacts.

"How long have they been at it?" I asked.

"Well, I got here at three forty-five, and they were already fighting then. So, over an hour now. When I came in, they were arguing about you."

"Me?"

"Yep. Paul was screaming about Steven's inappropriate behavior toward you and the way he ogles you. Steven was egging him on, shouting that Paul was in love with you, and he was going to get in your pants before Paul did and show you what a real man can do."

My stomach flipped thinking about Paul being in love with me. I gave myself a fraction of a second to consider it before pushing the thought away.

Don't go there, girl!

However, the thought of Steven getting in my pants made me nauseous.

"Barbi, please tell me you're joking."

Before she could answer, a loud crash came from the office. I looked at Barbi and handed her my bag.

"Stow this behind the bar, please. I'm going to put a stop to this. We should be opening soon."

I walked back to the office, paused at the waitress station, and grabbed two glasses of ice water. Pushing the door open with my foot, I discovered the two men taking swings at one another, oblivious to my presence. I walked to Steven and splashed an entire glass of ice water in his face. Only half of it made the target. The rest landed on his throat and shirt.

"What the fuck, Tula?"

"What the fuck? I should be asking you the same thing. First, we are unlocking the doors for customers in about ten minutes, so this fighting needs to end. Second, this shouting match has the staff freaked out. Third, if you even think about selling The Oyster, I will have you facing a legal battle so long that, by the time it's over, we'll all be thinking of retiring because you will never get control of my part of this place. And last but not least, hell will fucking freeze over before you get in my pants! Have I made myself clear?" Paul, who had stood silently as I ranted, laughed. I faced him, my back to Steven, squinted, and frowned. "Do you need this other glass? I brought two for a reason."

"No, ma'am."

He was trying hard to be serious, but holding back his laughter was impossible. His laugh caused me to widen my eyes as I rolled them and smiled at Paul as I drank from the glass. The cold water felt good on my dry throat after yelling at Steven.

As I walked toward the door, I said, "Okay, let's get moving. And, Steven, go grab a dry Oyster Bar T-shirt. You shouldn't be wearing that red Polo to work anyway. You look like a Target employee."

Steven growled, and Paul laughed. It was going to be a long night.

Every night, it seemed, something unexpected happened at The Oyster. There must have been a full moon that Thursday night, though. After the guys argued, the night spiraled out of control. Three members of the kitchen staff called out, a fryer stopped working, and Katy dropped an entire tray of steamed mussels on a busboy. Once the dinner rush was nearly over, I thought we would survive the night without further incident. And then Uncle Parker stumbled through the door.

The restaurant was still full of customers, and I was in the kitchen plating eight meals for a table. My head and my finger were throbbing when I heard a man screaming.

"You killed him! You fucking killed my son," the voice of my Uncle Parker echoed through the building. "You killed him! You'll go after Tula next. You want everybody dead so you can sell this place."

I raced out of the kitchen. I hit the swinging door so hard it swung back and smacked my shoulder as I moved into the dining area. I flinched as I looked around. My eyes settled on the bar, where my uncle stood inches away from Paul, jabbing Paul's chest with his finger.

"You're going to rot in hell! Dawson loved you like a brother, and you killed him!"

I dashed to the bar, placing myself between the two men, and let out a deep sigh. "Uncle Parker, let's take this conversation out to the dock. People don't want to listen to arguing while they eat."

"Says who?" He slurred his words as he spoke.

This was the drunkest I had seen him. Ever. I was shocked he could even stand up.

"Aunt Cookie. She and Mom both taught me that."

Paul stood silently. I had to give the man credit. It would have been my first instinct to defend myself, yelling and screaming in return, but he did not say a thing.

I grabbed Barbi by the arm as she walked by. When she stopped, I pulled my phone out of my back pocket and handed it to her. "Would you call my Aunt Cookie, please? Have her bring the car here."

"Why are you calling her, you little bitch?"

I was shocked to hear this come from my uncle's mouth. While I rarely agreed with him, he never spoke to me in a derogatory manner. I am not certain why, but I looked to

Paul as if I was seeking his guidance. What my eyes landed on was a seething, angry man with his gaze boring down on my uncle. He had not looked like that when I first stepped into the dining room.

Before either of us could speak, he reached around, gently pushing me behind him as he not so gently shoved Parker away from us. "That's where I draw the line. You will not disrespect Tula. She's too special to be treated like that."

This was the second time in one night he had defended my honor. It left me dumbstruck. Men did not do that. At least not any man I ever met, except for my father. My last ex would have said nothing and watched me struggle. Later, he would have admonished me for making a scene. He always made me feel like I was not good enough to be with him. However, Paul's behavior put me in a place of feeling cherished, and he didn't even know me.

I watched as Paul grabbed Parker's arm, basically dragging him out to the dock. I followed close behind, watching my uncle stumble, and trying to keep up with Paul's long strides.

When we were near the end of the dock, Paul stopped and turned to my uncle. "Let's get one thing straight. I did not kill Dawson. You're only right about one thing. We loved each other like brothers. I would have died for that man!"

"I wish you had!"

I knew my uncle was grieving, but he had gone too far one too many times. I sighed as I stepped up to Parker. My Aunt Cookie and Barbi's voices grew louder as they approached the dock.

"Uncle Parker, that's enough! Get control of yourself." I grabbed his arm to command his full attention.

I didn't realize how close to the edge of the dock he was standing. The next thing happened so quickly, there was no way anyone could have stopped it. My uncle lost his balance, fell backward, and grabbed my shoulders to steady himself. However, my slight size was no competition for the rate at which he was falling, and the next thing I knew, we both splashed into the water between two large boats docked by customers having dinner. We were lucky neither of us hit a boat as we fell. It could have been disastrous.

I took one look at my uncle treading water. He looked confused as if he had no clue how he had ended up in Connelly's Creek. I shook my head and swam away from the small channel of water between the boats when a customer yelled, "Use my boat to get back onto the dock!"

I swam to a boat, not knowing which one I had been invited to use. When I reached the ladder, I climbed up onto the boat's deck and used it to hop back onto the dock. As I stood, dripping wet, I saw my uncle still in the water. That's when Cookie said, "Oh, God, Parker. Are you too drunk to figure out how to get out of the water?"

I saw a life ring land in front of Parker with a rope attached to it. I followed the rope with my eyes and found Paul at the other end. He was standing on the boat closest to Parker, dragging him over to the ladder. When he reached it, Paul reached down and pulled him from the water.

When the men stepped off the boat, Paul left Parker for Cookie to manage and came directly to me. As he approached, I saw his lagoon-blue eyes brimming with concern. "Are you okay?"

"I'm good. Really. Luckily, the tide is high, so I didn't have far to fall." I looked over to the restaurant windows while I rang out my water-drenched hair. Paul reached up and pushed a few pieces of hair from my face.

"Where did this color come from, anyway? A box? Salon? There's no way that's your natural color."

I smiled. "My mother."

"Sorry. It's just so different."

"It's okay. My mother was a very special person, right down to the hair on her head." I looked to the restaurant once more, only to see everyone, guests and staff alike, with their attention solely on us. I sighed yet again. "I hate to leave with The Oyster being so busy, but I've got to go home and change."

"Take the rest of the night off if you want. You've had a crazy day. A crazy couple of days now that I think about it." As he spoke, he gently scooped up my hand, examining my finger protected by a waterproof latex finger sleeve.

We stood, frozen in time. It seemed like hours but was only a few seconds. I felt connected to him. I couldn't explain it, but it felt wonderfully warm and reassuring.

Don't let this happen. You know how these things end.

I blinked hard and slowly pulled my hand out of his. I looked at my watch, which was no longer functioning, then back at Paul. "I don't know what time it is, but I know the night is far from over. I'll be back in about twenty minutes." As I walked off the dock, I watched Cookie load her drunk husband into the car. I would probably need a new place to live come the morning. I climbed in the back of Cookie's car and headed home for a quick shower and change before walking back.

Chapter Twelve

Paul

I REPLAYED THE PREVIOUS night's dock incident. That moment, holding Tula's hand somehow fused me to her. I never experienced that with anyone. Not even my ex-wife. When the dock at my house came into view, I forced myself to focus on docking the boat and not this woman I found myself consumed by.

As I pulled the boat up to my dock, I glimpsed a golden retriever rounding the corner of my house. I didn't recognize this dog. The neighbors' dogs roamed along Main Street in Jett's Landing. They were all friendly, and I enjoyed their company. It was great for me. I had all the fun of owning a dog without the responsibility. The dog trotted over to the beach and splashed into the water. He swam around to cool off from the summer heat and was making his way back to shore when a familiar yelled, "George? Where are you? George, bark."

Surprisingly, the dog barked. I quickly tied up the boat as I watched the dog with great curiosity.

"George, again." The dog barked once more and then jumped out of the water and ran until he reached a person rounding the corner. The person was Tula. "What are you doing over here, you crazy dog?"

As she spoke, George shook the bay water from his fur, showering Tula. I held back my amusement until I could not resist. However, she seemed unaware of my presence.

"Really, George? I'm going to have to grab a dry shirt when I get to work. I don't think The Oyster is the kind of place that has wet T-shirt contests, and this was my last clean shirt. The rest are still on the line at Aunt Cookie's house, drying."

"No, but it's not a bad idea. Tuesday nights are slow. We could try it then," I said, jokingly. When I spoke, Tula jumped, not realizing I was standing on the dock next to the sandy, man-made area. "Sorry, didn't mean to startle you."

"It's okay. I startle easily. Always have."

"Is this going to be your new thing? Every time I see you, you're going to be wearing a wet T-shirt?"

"No," she said with a smirk and a head shake as I laughed. "I hope not. What has you at the Fisher House today, anyway?"

"I own it."

"No kidding?" She sighed.

I noticed she did this whenever she wished things were different. She had done it the first night she worked when we talked about our heights or lack thereof. It happened again the night she sliced her finger open, and there was a lot of sighing going on the previous night concerning her uncle.

"You're wishing I didn't own it?" I asked.

"No, it's just that this is the house I've always dreamed of owning. When it was last on the market—I guess that would be when you bought it—I had just bought my place in the Keys. I didn't have the funds to buy it. I don't know what I would have done with it even if I had. My life isn't here." Tula looked at her new watch, and her eyes expanded to twice their normal size. "I've got to get moving, or I'm going to be late."

She looked at George, who sat at her feet as we talked, watching us like a tennis match. Tula leaned down until she was eye-to-eye with the retriever. "George, you need to apologize for showing up uninvited to Paul's beach and go home."

George looked at me, knowing he had done something wrong. His goofy dog smile was gone, and his ears hung low. He looked back at Tula, and she tilted her head toward me.

"Woof" fell out of his mouth.

I had never seen a dog trained to respond like this. It was amazing. I walked up next to him and knelt. The three of us were now on the same level.

"George, you are always welcome here."

I don't know how much he understood, but when I said the word welcome, he stood, wagging his tail, and shaking his butt as his smile returned and ears perked up. I patted his head before scratching an ear. Tula reached over and rubbed his other ear.

"Are you sure you don't mind? He's so spoiled. But that's my doing. He tends to act like he owns everything everywhere he goes. And at home, it's pretty much the truth."

As she spoke, I gazed into her eyes. This time, I noticed gray mini-starbursts in three spots on each eye. They hid in her olive irises, only visible in the bright sunlight. I avoided her at work sometimes because of those eyes. I was beginning to believe Tula was a siren and that my doom was inevitable.

As we gave George the affection he deserved, our hands kept finding each other's, intertangling in his fur. The pace of her breathing increased, and her eyes locked on mine. I could see her mind racing behind them. After a minute, she blinked, breaking the connection, and standing.

"Well, I should go. Are you on the schedule tonight?"

"Yes, but not until later. Why are you heading in so early? The produce truck?"

"Yep, I better hustle, too, or the driver is going to be sitting there pissed."

"Wait, isn't that Glenn's job this week?"

"Yeah, but no one has seen him in two days, and if we want broccoli tonight, I figured I better go in."

"We're that low on broccoli?" She nodded. "Glenn really is a decent guy. His wife left him recently, and I don't think he's taking it well. I've been trying to cut him a little slack, but if he keeps this up, I'll have to say something."

Tula nodded again and turned her attention to her dog.

"George, be a good boy." She leaned over, and he gave her a slobbery kiss on the cheek. She stood and turned away before stopping. "Hey, Paul, thanks for your help with Uncle Parker last night. I've never seen him that drunk nor that angry."

"Is he mad at you? I've got five unused bedrooms if you need to relocate while the dust settles."

"Thanks, but he doesn't even remember what happened. He said the last thing he remembered was thinking he should go to the restaurant and give you a piece of his mind. And the next thing he knew the sun was rising, and he was asleep in the hammock in the backyard, smelling like creek water and covered in mosquito bites."

"He didn't make it to his bed before passing out?"

"No, Aunt Cookie forbade him from entering the house until he sobered up. I've never seen her so mad in my life. She made him apologize to me even though he doesn't remember what he did."

I was half hoping Parker was mad at her so she would take one of my rooms. I craved the opportunity to spend more time with her. The idea of her under my roof was intoxicating.

"Well, I was happy to help. But if I ever hear about him treating you like that again, I won't be as nice." She stared back at me, looking confused. I was beginning to think she didn't understand her own worth. "I didn't like the way he spoke to you."

"Oh," she said, still confused, until her dog barked. She shook her head in what appeared to be an effort to clear her thoughts. "Thanks for letting George hang out. I think he's a little lonely here."

"Anytime." Her dog sat next to me, leaning against my leg. "The same goes for you, too. Feel free to use my beach whenever you'd like."

"Thanks," she said with a dazzling smile. "I will definitely take you up on that. I've got a day off coming up soon. Well, see you later."

We both watched Tula walk away. I did not know what the dog was looking at, but I could not take my eyes off her ass. I would be lying if I said this was the first time I had stared at it. It made me wonder if George was the only lonely visitor from Key West and what I could do to get her in my bed as well as my life. I wouldn't give up until I found a way.

Chapter Thirteen

Tula

IT WAS ONLY NINE in the morning, but it was sweltering. I was up all night, writing, and gave up on sleep at around six in the morning. It had been a productive writing session, and my articles for the newspaper at home were prepared for the next two weeks.

My editor, Roger Gray, had been understanding when I told him I would need to expand my leave of absence from Key West but could keep writing my column. I kept a backlog of generic articles for the island's paper in case of emergencies. It was the advantage of writing for the lifestyle section. I had about three weeks' worth of articles sitting in a file on my computer. However, they wouldn't last long, so I was trying not to use them all at once.

I watched from the window of Dawson's room as George trotted across the street. He headed toward Paul's beach. George was smart. It was the perfect day to be in the water.

I threw on my green bikini, a pair of cut-off jeans, and an old Jimmy Buffett T-shirt. I filled a tote bag with a bottle of water, a towel, and some sunscreen. I threw my phone and Kindle in a Ziplock bag before adding them to the tote while I searched for a missing flip-flop. It was underneath George's bed.

Cookie purchased the giant dog bed with an orthopedic memory foam mattress when we extended our stay. She spent hours researching dog beds online and had it delivered via FedEx, so it would arrive quickly. George previously was content sleeping at the foot of my bed or on the floor, but now, his dog bed was his favorite place to lounge.

Mornings along the water were always my favorite. As the sun shone on the waves, it created a show resembling tiny flickering lights. Paul's beach was a little slice of heaven showcasing those lights. It was quiet and tucked away behind the house, so it was not visible from the road. Someone had taken the time to landscape the area around it when it was a bed-and-breakfast, and it was well maintained. Beautiful shrubs and flowers were tucked next to large rocks and driftwood. I noticed there was no clothesline in the backyard. Clotheslines were still a staple in Jett's Landing. There's nothing like fresh sheets straight from a clothesline on a bed.

A loud splash pulled me away from my thoughts of laundry, and I smiled as I watched George swim around, chasing a piece of seaweed floating in the water. I took the time to shove my discarded T-shirt and shorts into my bag and thoroughly applied sunscreen.

Stretching out in one of Paul's Adirondack chairs, I closed my eyes. My senses were flooded with the strong aroma of brackish water and the warmth of sunshine. I listened to the waves breaking on the shore mixed with the ringing of the wind chimes hanging next to his screened-in porch. They weren't high and tinny like small chimes but deep and melodic. The hypnotic Zen-like bells were relaxing.

I was almost asleep when I heard Paul clear his throat and my eyes popped open and remained wide.

"Good morning."

"Hey, Paul. I hope you don't mind. You said I was welcome to use your beach."

"I don't mind at all. I thought you might like some orange juice." He handed me a glass of ice-cold juice, and I took a sip.

It was freshly squeezed. He sat in the chair next to me and watched George as he drank the juice he brought out for himself.

It was obvious he had just rolled out of bed. His hair was a mess, and his beard needed a trim. He was wearing swim trunks and a T-shirt. Except for the one dress shirt, I was beginning to think he owned nothing but Oyster Bar T-shirts and his choice of clothing had yet to prove me wrong.

"I think I'm going to take Calliope out. You and George want to come?"

"You're going to date the Greek muse of eloquence, and you want George and I to double date with you?" I asked with a mischievous grin.

"I love that you know my boat was named after a Greek muse and what she represents," he said, smiling. His smile could light up a room. "So, do you want to go for a ride?"

"Paul, I don't want you to feel like you need to entertain me. I just thought a little fresh air and sunshine would do me good."

"I'm taking the boat out either way. It's just more fun when I've got company. Come on, let's go."

I downed my orange juice, smiled, and grabbed my bag. "Come on, George. We're going on a boat ride."

Chapter Fourteen

Paul

TULA SAT AT the bow of my boat as I sped across the water. The warm wind blew a few strands of hair that escaped her ponytail across her face. George sat next to her, and she rubbed his ear as she smiled. She looked peaceful. It was as if she was meant to live this life. Tula grew up bouncing from one military base to another, but she was well suited for life on the water.

I slowed the boat as we approached the Smith Point lighthouse. There were three lighthouses in the area, but this was my favorite. It was not on land but built over the water about two miles from the shore. I killed the engine and dropped the anchor. She watched a random crab pot marker bob from the wake caused by the boat before she stood.

"It's gorgeous here," she said as she walked over to where I was standing. "Thanks for bringing me out."

"Anytime. Do you have a boat in Key West?"

"No. Too expensive. The docking fees are out of my budget and the water is too shallow to dock a boat at my house."

"Your place is on the water?"

"Yes. It's not a lot of beach, but it's nice."

I watched her as she talked about her home. The corners of her lips turned down. As soon as she realized she was no longer smiling, she closed her eyes, took a deep breath, smiled, and reopened her olive-green eyes. The gold flecks in them caught the sunlight, and she looked ethereal.

"You miss home, don't you?"

"Yeah, but I'm glad I'm here. I think Cookie needs me right now. After all she's done for me, it's the least I can do."

"Why do I have the feeling there's a story there?" I moved over to the cooler I placed on the boat before leaving and pulled out two Cokes. I tossed one over to Tula and opened the other for myself as I sat on the bench on the port side of the boat. She sat across from me on the starboard side.

"She moved in with us when my mom was dying of cancer. I'm a lot younger than my sisters. They were already out of the house, and Dad was focusing all of his attention on Mom. Cookie made sure I got to school on time, cooked dinner for me and Dad every night, took me shopping for my prom dress, and all those things Mom would have done."

"That's unimaginable for me. To be so young and have to deal with that." I watched as a wave of sadness moved across her face.

There was no doubt in my mind that she missed her mom. It was time for me to change the subject.

"Let's raise anchor and head over to The Sulfur Flats."

"The Sulfur Flats?"

"Yeah. It's a shallow area not too far of a ride from here. You can get out and wade around. It does something to your skin. You might smell a little like sulfur until you get a shower but your skin will never feel better."

While we spoke, I raised the anchor and started the engine. I knew she'd like this place.

It didn't take long to get there, and when I cut the engine and dropped anchor, Tula wrinkled her nose. "You can definitely smell it."

"It's actually not too bad today. The breeze helps."

"This is supposed to be good for your skin?"

"It is. Just trust me." I hopped out first and then stood by for assistance as she made her way down the ladder.

She didn't need it. We were standing next to each other and the water was just above waist-high on me and nearly armpit-high on her. She must have seen me smile and realized I was looking at our differences in height.

"Don't say a word."

My smile grew. "I wasn't going to."

"Smart man."

The next thing I heard was a big splash as George jumped from the boat. He swam around, enjoying the water, and stood in the areas that were extra shallow.

We walked around in the water until we found the perfect spot to sit. We were up to our necks in water. I was sitting, but Tula was standing on her knees.

"I just realized I did all the talking at the lighthouse. Tell me more about you," she said.

"Like what?"

"I don't know. Do you have siblings? Are your parents still alive?"

She was honestly curious about me. Maybe it was a good sign that I wasn't the only one feeling this connection.

"My mom is. She still lives in Ohio. I keep trying to convince her to move out here, but she likes where she is, and my brother lives close by with his wife and kids. She gets to see my nephews almost every day."

"What about your dad?"

"Don't know. He took off when my mom was pregnant with my brother, and I was three. I don't really remember much about him."

"I'm sorry. I don't know what my life would be like if my dad wasn't part of it. I'll be the first to admit that I'm a Daddy's Girl."

"It's kind of obvious," I said, smiling. "It's actually quite endearing."

"A lot of guys didn't think so when I was younger. Most never went out with me more than once because of it. Especially if they were in the Air Force when they found out my dad was The Colonel. When I was seventeen one guy, who was eighteen and fresh out of basic, asked me out constantly for over a month before I agreed to go to the movies with him. When he came to pick me up, Dad opened the front door and the guy didn't say a word. He turned around, got into his car, and drove away."

I chuckled, and she smiled. We sat a little longer, enjoying the peace and quiet. I looked at my watch and frowned. "Unfortunately, I have to be at the restaurant in a couple of hours, so we should probably head home."

Chapter Fifteen

Paul

TULA GOT GEORGE close to the ladder before she realized she couldn't get him on board. Getting back in a boat by himself was a skill George had yet to learn. She was an independent woman who would not ask for help. I took two steps to where George was, lifted him out of the water, and slung him over one shoulder before climbing up the ladder and depositing him on the floor of the boat.

"Dude, you have got to cut back on your snacks. You weigh a ton."

Of course, the only word George understood was snacks, so he wagged his tail. I turned back to the ladder to see Tula climbing it. I reached over and gave her my hand for support as she got on board. When I did, I noticed a faded but substantial scar under her left shoulder blade that wrapped around and disappeared under her arm. Whatever caused it must have been traumatic.

Tula was spectacular in her green bikini. It looked like it had been custom-made for her. As tiny as she was, I could only imagine how hard it was to find clothes that fit. I had a similar problem because of my long legs and arms.

As I stared at her, I noticed her shoulders were getting red. I didn't want to let go of her hand, but I did. I wanted to hold that hand forever.

"Your shoulders are getting crispy. Is there a shirt in your bag?"

"Yeah, I've got one." She grabbed her bag and put her T-shirt on. "You're right about this place. My skin has never felt so soft."

Tula hadn't dried off before pulling her shirt on, and within seconds, it was wet.

"Another wet T-shirt?" I grinned.

Tula laughed quietly as she shook her head and rolled her eyes. She took some sunscreen out of her bag and reapplied it to her arms and face.

"Wanna take her back?"

"You want me to drive?" She looked uneasy. "I've never been behind the wheel of anything but a car."

"Don't worry, I'll guide you through it."

I gave her a quick lesson on how the Boston Whaler operated and what the controls did. After she sat in the captain's chair, George trotted over to Tula and made himself at home, lying next to her before quickly drifting off to sleep. I raised the anchor, and she slowly headed back toward my house.

When we hit deep, open water, I encouraged Tula to open the throttle and hit full speed. She was hesitant. After a few minutes, I walked up behind her and leaned in to increase the speed.

I was so close to her I could smell the sunscreen on her skin. I knew the brand. It was the one a high school girlfriend used whenever we were at her father's pool. I could not remember the girl's name, but the scent was as intoxicating as it had been all those years ago.

"Hawaiian Tropic?" I whispered into her ear, doubting she even heard me.

I had not intended to do so, but my mouth brushed against her ear. I felt her body shiver before her muscles visibly tensed.

"It's my favorite. I can't seem to find it around here, though. I had to order it online."

I made a note to myself to order some to keep on the boat. I wanted her to have it for whenever I could get her out for a ride.

You're awfully confident she likes you.

After a few minutes, she relaxed and enjoyed driving the boat. As the dock came into view, I remembered something I didn't think she knew.

"Tula, slow up a little. The water is about to get shallow again and there are a bunch of underwater obstacles around here."

There were shallow spots, a long sandbar, and a skiff that sank a few weeks earlier when a bunch of drunk teenage boys decided it would be a smart idea to set off fireworks from the boat. It caught fire and sank. Luckily, they swam to shore. One of them was the sheriff's son, so I was certain they were not arrested, either.

"You want to take over?" she asked.

"Nope. When we get to that marker, turn right." I pointed toward the nearby post displaying a triangular sign. "We're going to skip all of this and dock at The Oyster."

"Oh, okay. You'll dock her when we get there, though, right?"

"No. You can do it. I'll talk you through it."

When we approached the restaurant, Tula asked, "Do you have time for a quick detour? I'd like to get a closer look at The Stack."

The Stack was visible, but I knew what she meant. She wanted to get a better look at the restoration.

"Absolutely."

She slowly made her way the short distance to where the smokestack was most visible, careful not to create a wake in the creek. She knew more about boating than she would admit to. I was learning she did not feed off of constant praise, so I said nothing.

Tula killed the engine, and I dropped the anchor. She sat and stared at the historic monument while I watched her. She was mesmerized by the men working on the high scaffolding. I was mesmerized by her.

We both sat, each looking at our current interest, for about five minutes before she turned to me and sighed.

"I guess we should go. I don't want you to be late."

"Yeah," I said. "I could sit here all day."

She looked back up at The Stack. "Me too."

We were talking about watching two different things, but she seemed oblivious to what I was doing. After I raised the anchor, Tula started the engine and carefully turned my boat around, heading toward the restaurant.

Her eyes were as big as saucers as we approached the dock. I guided her through it all, and Tula put Calliope exactly where she needed to be tied up. She breathed a sigh of relief once it was done.

"Good job, but I think George isn't ready to leave yet." We looked down to see the retriever fast asleep. I smiled. "Leave him. When he wakes up, he'll make his way to the restaurant, and I'll make sure he gets home. Why don't you come in? I'll make us some lunch. I'm starving."

"Me too. I'll help if you want."

We made our way into the restaurant, and Tula dropped her bag onto the bar but not before grabbing her shorts from it and slipping them on over the bottoms of her bikini. I headed to the kitchen, and she followed.

We worked together, and within fifteen minutes, we were sitting in the restaurant alone eating fried scallops and French fries. It was more grease than I normally ingested in a meal, but it was quick, and I was hungry.

As we ate, we talked. We talked about the restaurant, what she thought of it now that she had been working a couple of weeks, and if she had any concerns. Her biggest issue was understanding how the partnership worked, as it had never been fully explained to her.

When we talked about the guys, I felt compelled to let Tula know what I had recently heard.

"So, I heard some people talking in the grocery store yesterday before I came to work. There's a rumor floating around about Glenn."

"You don't sound pleased about it. What did you hear?"

"The rumor is that when Glenn disappears, he's running drugs from Key West to Delaware. I don't know if there is any truth behind it but if I wasn't worried about him before, I certainly am now. I'm going to talk with him tonight." I could almost see the gears turning inside her head. "What are you thinking?"

"When I met Glenn, I thought I recognized him, but I couldn't place him. Is it possible I saw him in Key West?" She shook her head "No, probably not. I've got an overactive imagination."

As we ate, we contemplated the rumor surrounding Glenn. We were finishing lunch when my curiosity got the best of me.

"Tula, do you mind if I ask how you ended up with the scar on your back?"

She looked up from her plate with kind eyes. "That's an unusually polite way to ask about it. Most people usually say something like, *Oh my God, that scar is hideous. What happened to you?*"

"Wow, that's rude. Who would say that?"

"My ex. Of course, he was a plastic surgeon. But to answer your question, I had emergency surgery when I was a baby."

She popped a scallop in her mouth and looked down, intentionally stopping the discussion. This was truly a sensitive topic for her. I shouldn't have brought it up, but I was shocked her ex, whoever the asshole was, would say something so insensitive especially when it wasn't that bad.

"I bet you were a cute baby," I said to her with a smile.

"Not really. I know all babies are supposed to be beautiful, but I was not."

"Not all babies are cute. My nephews were ugly little space aliens." She laughed at my comment before I continued. "But you had to be lovely."

"Why?"

"Because you're beautiful now. And beautiful women don't start out as ugly babies. It's a fact."

She looked stunned, like no man had ever told her she was beautiful.

She swallowed hard before replying. It was as if she needed to search for her voice, which was just above a whisper. "Fact? You have evidence to support this?"

I was trying to come up with something witty to say when the doorbell at the delivery door rang.

"He's early," I said, instead of a clever comment.

"Who?"

"The guy that owns The Baker's Dozen Brewing Company. He wanted to deliver our first order from there in person. He owns part of Thomas Hall Winery, too. The place we get our wine from. His name is Henry Baker."

"Nice play on his name with The Baker's Dozen."

"Nice guy, too. Come meet him." As I stood, I watched as she looked down as if she had just remembered she was in a still wet T-shirt.

"Go let him in. I'm just going to go grab a dry Oyster Bar shirt, and I'll be right behind you."

When Tula made her way back to the dining area, we were at the bar, loading the beer into a display fridge. She sat on one of the bar stools. I looked up, glimpsed hesitant eyes, and smiled hoping to ease whatever discomfort this situation brought her.

"Henry, this is Tula Yates. Tula, Henry Baker."

Henry extended his hand, and she did the same.

"It's been a long time," Tula said. "I didn't make the connection when Paul mentioned your name."

"All I knew was that Dawson's cousin was here. I didn't realize you were that cousin. I'm sorry I missed the funeral. We were away at a baseball tournament my son was in."

"Wait," I said, bewildered. "Two things. First, how did the tournament go? And second, you two know each other?"

"Sam pitched well. His team won the tournament. And yes, we know each other, but it's been what? Five years? The last time we saw each other was at—"

"The wedding." Tula looked like she was about to be sick. She closed her eyes, sighed, and plastered a smile on her face before changing the subject. "So, what yummy things did you bring us to drink?"

I watched as the two talked about beer and knew there was more to their last encounter than mentioned. How could a wedding stir up so much distraught emotion in Tula?

Chapter Sixteen

Tula

IT WAS ALMOST FOUR thirty and no sign of Steven. I had no idea what I was doing. I would not survive the night in charge. I hadn't been at The Oyster long enough to know everything that needed to be done. I pulled out my phone but then hesitated. Ever since our boat ride and conversation two days earlier, I felt a little nervous about the prospect of talking to Paul. I even talked to Aunt Cookie about it, which is not something I would normally do. I knew I would have to talk to him eventually, though. After all, we worked together most days.

I dialed a number and Paul answered on the first ring. "Hi, Tula. You know it's my day off, right?"

"I know, and I'm sorry. Steven isn't here yet and I'm freaking out. There's a ton of stuff I don't know how to do, and all the employees keep asking me questions I don't have answers for. I tried calling his house, but his wife said he left before she woke up this morning, and his cell is going straight to voicemail."

"I'm guessing Glenn is still MIA?"

"Yeah. It's really annoying that he floats in and out of here while the rest of us are working our asses off."

"I know. It bugs me, too. Give me a few minutes. I just got home from getting groceries. Let me put them away, and I'll walk down to The Oyster."

"Thanks. Again, I'm really sorry. I know it sucks to come in on your day off."

"Quit apologizing. It's not your fault. I think it is time, however, for you to learn everything so you can run the place."

Chapter Seventeen

Tula

E SURVIVED THE DINNER rush. It hadn't been a busy night. The thunderstorms punctuating the evening's serenity kept most of the locals at home. There were a few customers still at tables, the kitchen staff was cleaning the kitchen, and I was standing at the hostess stand when a gorgeous blonde walked through the door. The woman finished folding her umbrella and left it by a coat rack near the entrance. She was close to six feet tall and had long straight, shiny hair parted down the center and legs for days.

I put my customer service smile on as she approached. "Welcome to The Oyster Bar & Grill. How can I help you?"

She looked down at me and smiled back. "You must be new. Is Paul around?"

"He's in the office. Let me get him for you."

"That's okay. I know the way."

I watched as she walked down the hall and went into the office, closing the door behind her. Why did I not know that Paul had a girlfriend? I thought we had a connection but maybe not. It didn't matter anyway. I would never get involved in another relationship again.

Katy walked over to the hostess stand and used it to lean against. She always showed a lot of skin when she dressed for work, and this night was no exception. If her shorts were any shorter, her butt cheeks would be exposed.

"Great, Linda's here," she said, sarcasm permeating her voice. "Get ready. Paul's mood is going to suck for about a week."

"Why? She seems nice enough."

"She is. She's also Paul's ex-wife. I got the impression that he was crushed when she left him. Every time she's close by, she stops in. His mood is always shit after she's been here."

I was strangely relieved to discover Linda was not Paul's girlfriend.

"What happened?" I asked.

"I'm not sure. He never talks about it. I didn't even know he had been married for the first six months I worked here."

I pondered this new information before organizing the hostess stand. It was then the office door opened and Paul followed Linda to where Katy and I stood. There was something hesitant in his movement. As though he were walking through a minefield. Sadness reflected in his eyes as well. They didn't look clear but a dark murky blue. I did not know Paul well, but something was definitely not normal.

"Katy, you remember Linda?" Katy nodded, turned, and headed to a table ready for their bill.

Paul was standing beside me with a nervous smile plastered on his face and slid his arm around me. When he did, his hands found bare skin. I had gotten into the habit of tying my T-shirts at the waist to shorten them so they didn't look like dresses on me.

"Babe, this is Linda, my ex. Linda this is Tula Yates. Dawson was her cousin."

Babe? Seriously?

I blinked hard, trying to comprehend what he said.

"I'm so sorry for your loss. Dawson was a great guy. I was sorry to miss the funeral, but I was in Boston on business."

As Linda spoke, Paul pulled me closer and pressed his lips against my temple. I did not know people showed affection like that except in movies. Why didn't I know this? And then I remembered why. Or should I say who?

That was the moment I understood what he was doing. I had a split second to decide whether I would play along, and if I did not, whether I would call him out on it.

"Thank you. He was a great guy. Probably my best friend, although we hadn't seen each other much these last few years," I said before turning to Paul. "I should probably go check the shrimp supply for tomorrow's order." I pressed my body into him, stood on my toes, wrapped my arms around his neck as he leaned down, and gave him a sweet peck of a kiss on the lips.

God, his arms feel good around me. Stop it! Bad idea, Tula!

"It was nice to meet you," I politely said, turning back to Linda. Then I walked through the kitchen doors and back to the storage room.

It was not until I was inside the room did I exhale. I sat there, thinking about the last few minutes. I should have been furious at Paul for using me like that. But I wasn't. He needed me, a friend, to get him through something, and I was happy to be there for him. But why did I kiss him? Had I lost my mind? About five minutes passed before there was a knock on the door. Paul did not wait for a reply but let himself in, closed the door, and sat on the produce box across from me.

He opened his mouth to say something. I tried to stop him but was unsuccessful. "I'm sorry. I shouldn't have done that to you. Linda just came in to tell me she's getting married again. She didn't want me to hear it from anyone else and said it didn't seem right to drop it into a text. I think she really wanted to make sure I would be okay when I heard the news."

"Are you?"

He paused. "I think I am. But then she asked me if I was seeing anyone. I didn't want her to think I was still alone. We've stayed friends, in spite of everything that happened, and she's been pushing me to get back into the dating scene."

"You don't need to explain yourself. I get it. If my ex ever shows up here, and you're close by, I'll probably introduce you as the father of my unborn child."

He smirked as a quiet chuckle escaped his lips. "You'd better introduce me as your husband, then. My fake, unborn child will not come into this world out of wedlock."

"So, no fake child support, huh?" I laughed, and he joined me.

I watched the thin lines form around his eyes. Sometimes I forgot he was older than me, not by too much, but the seven years was enough to see the difference. Our expressions transitioned into something different. His went from laughter to seriousness and then to something that, if I did not know better, resembled lust or maybe even longing.

"Paul, this is a bad idea." I stood, and he followed, keeping our eyes locked. He reached down, intending to put his hand on my cheek. Just then, the storage room door opened. I froze, knowing this could start rumors. Paul saw the panicked expression on my face, reached up to the top shelf, retrieved a box, and handed it to me.

"There you go, Munchkin," he said, winking at me as he handed me the box.

"Tula, there's a call out front for you," Katy said, letting the light from the kitchen hold her in silhouette. "She said she's your sister, Lily. I didn't know you had a sister."

"I have several, but Lily is the only one that lives close by." As I spoke, he watched as I placed the case of carry-out boxes on top of the produce box I was previously sitting on and headed to the door. Katy smiled when she let me pass, then said, "Paul, that was lame. Especially for you. Don't use Tula like that again. I don't like when people use my friends."

Chapter Eighteen

Paul

BY THE NEXT MORNING, the police formally declared Steven missing. His wife, Peggy, wanted to file a missing person's report the day before but was advised to wait twenty-four hours. The police decided to conveniently show up to interview the staff at the restaurant during the dinner rush.

Tula was waiting tables for each waitress as they were interviewed by the officer assigned to the case, Neil Weston. I watched her on the office monitor as she continued to help the waitresses while Officer Weston interviewed me.

"Do you know of anyone who had a problem with Steven?"

"Honestly, I did and so did a lot of other people. I've had some complaints in the last few years by women concerning his behavior."

"Why don't you like him, and who are these women?"

"My problem with him is the way he treats women. He acts like they are all disposable idiots. As for the women who complained, he was flirting inappropriately and didn't know when to stop. One was a customer. We comped her dinner. She seemed to enjoy the food, but she never returned. A couple of waitresses complained to me, and I spoke to Steven about it. Neither work here anymore. When the summer ended last year, they both left and went to work for the Mexican restaurant in the next county over."

"Anyone else?"

"Have you talked to Tula yet?"

"The new girl? No, not yet."

"She's not a new girl. She's Dawson's cousin and our new partner."

"What's her relationship like with Steven? We all know Steven runs around on Peggy."

"There isn't one. Less than a month after being here, she asked me to make sure he was never in a room alone with her."
"What happened?"

"I don't know the details, but I told her if she felt uncomfortable around him, I'd make sure they were never alone."

"Why don't we get her in here? I want to hear from this girl about the argument between you and Steven that she witnessed."

"Neil, quit calling her this girl. Her name is Tula."

"It's Detective Weston when I'm on the clock."

"It's me treating you with the same respect you're treating her. I'll be right back."

I walked into the dining room to see Tula holding Anna Haynie's baby and playing with him. She did this sometimes so a mom could enjoy her meal while it was hot.

She will make a fantastic mother someday.

When I reached the two, looking at the fish tank by the bar, the little boy reached out to me, and I instinctively took him. It reminded me I had not talked to my nephews in a while.

"The detective wants to talk to both of us. Go on into the office, and I'll return the little tyke to his mom."

She stood there like a statue, smiling.

"You're great with kids. You'd make a good dad."

"You'd make a great mom, too. You make it look easy," I said as I was now bouncing the restless child. "I'll be there in a minute."

Tula headed down the hall, and I quickly returned Anna's son back to her. She was just finishing the last clam on her plate and was thankful for the break.

When I walked into the office, Tula was telling the detective about her first encounter with Steven.

"I told Paul a vague version of what happened, but it wasn't like he attacked me. It was just inappropriate and creepy. Especially since he's married."

"How long have you known he was married? Did you know then?"

"Of course, I did. He wears a wedding ring. Detective, I see where this is going so, I'm going to save you some time. I don't date married men. For that matter, I don't date at all. I have no interest in Steven. He gave off enough creepy, bad energy that I asked Paul to make sure I was never alone with him, and I haven't been since."

I sat next to her, and he continued to ask questions.

"Tell me your version of the argument that you witnessed between Steven and Paul."

"I really didn't witness much. I came in late that day. I forgot to set an alarm and overslept. When I got here, I could hear them in the office arguing as soon as I walked in the door. I asked Barbi what was going on, and she told me they were arguing about me earlier. I handed her my bag, grabbed a couple of glasses of ice water, went into the office, and poured one on Steven. It worked well enough that by the time I was done yelling at him and admonishing Paul, I didn't need the second glass for either of them."

"So, you didn't hear the part about you at all?"

"No, I just heard the part about selling the restaurant. Steven wants to sell, and Paul doesn't."

"What about you?"

"It's no secret that I'd sell my part to the right person at the right time, but I won't allow it to be sold off to a land developer that wants to level it." I knew she wanted to go home to Key West, but the idea of her selling her part of the restaurant still stung. "This place meant a lot to my cousin, and I would never do anything I think disrespects his memory."

Detective Weston stood and handed us each a card. "I think I've got what I need for now. If you think of anything, let me know."

"Is there anything new on my cousin's murder?" Tula asked, stopping him from leaving.

He turned to Tula. "We're still waiting on the forensics lab to send their report. Unfortunately, we haven't found the murder weapon. The coroner is certain it was a serrated kitchen knife. My guess is that it's somewhere out in the creek, making it impossible to find. I'll let your aunt and uncle know when we have something new."

"Okay. Thanks."

"I just realized that you're the person that emailed me your statement concerning talking to Dawson the night he died. You're a long way from home."

"I am. I wasn't sure if it would help at all, but I figured you should probably know everything he said."

"We should talk more about it sometime soon," he said.

"My cell number is on that email. Call me anytime."

The detective smiled but not before scanning her from head to toe. I didn't like it.

"It was nice meeting you, ma'am." He shook her hand.

"You too. Have you had any dinner? We'd be glad to put an order in for you."

"Maybe another time."

After he made his way to the door, I turned to Tula. "You spoke to him the night he died?"

"Yeah. He started telling me this crazy story that he'd done something when he was young and was certain he was about to go to jail. He sounded scared. He was about to tell me what happened when I heard a door slam on his end of the line, and he said he would call me the next day. He never did."

I watched Tula fight back tears. The sad expression was heartbreaking. She and Dawson had been close. When we were in college, they talked a few times a week, and this hadn't changed over the years. I was certain they talked or texted almost daily until his death.

"I should probably go check the dining room and make sure everything is okay," she said as she headed through the office door. Before she reached it, she faced me. "The Fourth of July is coming up soon. Where are the decorations stored?"

"We don't have any. Steven and Glenn thought they were tacky and a waste of money."

"As an Air Force brat, that doesn't work for me. Don't worry about it, though. I'll take care of it."

I glanced at the calendar. Independence Day was less than a week away. I pulled the schedule from the corkboard to rework it. Glenn was his normal missing in action self and Steven was actually missing. The busiest weekend of the year, and it would probably only be Tula and me running the place. I knew she would do her part, but it would be a hell of a week.

Chapter Nineteen

Paul

THE DINERS AND STAFF made their way out to the dock to watch the Fourth of July fireworks over the creek. Shawncy and Tula had come in earlier than usual and decorated the outdoor dining area and dock with red, white, and blue paper lanterns, American flags and patriotic bunting. It was the most festive I had ever seen the restaurant look on Independence Day. I couldn't stop smiling after I saw it.

The night sky burst with spectacular lights in rapid succession. White, crimson, bright blue, and gold illuminated the shoreline in flashes and the water multiplied the light show by mirroring the pyrotechnics below. Everyone was outside watching. Everyone but Tula.

I was on the outdoor dining deck with some of the others, standing near the back, by the entrance to the bar when I first heard the clanking of dishes and saw Tula working inside. I watched her as she cleared away any obviously empty plates and refilled drinks. She seemed to enjoy occasionally looking up at the colorful glow the fireworks created, but the sound disturbed her as she flinched with every explosion.

Spotlights at the base of The Stack illuminated the now scaffolding-free structure. It looked amazing with the brightly colored pyrotechnics behind it.

I walked back into the restaurant. "You know, you could take a break and watch the fireworks."

"That's okay. I'm not a big fan of them. Too loud. The sound of them has bothered me for a long time."

"Any particular reason?"

"When I was a kid, I witnessed a massive fireworks explosion one Fourth of July on a military base. The first one went straight up and came straight back down. It landed on the barge with the fireworks for the entire show before it exploded. Everything went off at once and within seconds it was engulfed in flames. The guy in charge of the display died. I've never gotten over the sounds from that night."

"So, take a break and watch from here. The lights are fantastic." I motioned her over to where I was standing. She hesitantly followed my suggestion and joined me by the window. I took the glass out of her hand and placed it on the table. As I did, a loud boom resonated from the fireworks and Tula jumped. I put my arm around her but kept my grip loose.

"The noise bothers you that much?" Tula nodded and pushed herself a little harder into me with the next explosion of sound. "Why didn't you say something? You could have taken the night off."

She turned and looked into my eyes. The dimmed lights in the restaurant made them almost dark gray and not olive. I wanted so much more from her, but I already knew she would probably never let her guard down. The walls she built around her heart could withstand a hurricane. But I would keep trying. I wasn't ready to give up yet.

"No, I couldn't have taken the night off. It's too busy and short-staffed in here tonight. But thank you."

"For what?" I asked, confused.

Tula's countenance changed. It was gentle and unguarded. If I thought she was beautiful before, it was only because I had never seen her with such a soft expression.

"For caring enough to offer."

I knew it was now or never. I had to do something. The plan I quickly formed in my head was either going to be a massive success or an epic failure. I put my free hand under her chin and cupped her face.

"I do care about you," I whispered.

I brushed her bottom lip with my thumb and felt her pulse race under my hand as I slowly leaned in to kiss her. I hesitated for a moment, licking my lips, and giving her a chance to pull away.

But she didn't. Instead, she rested the weight of her head in my hand and whispered something about this being a bad idea as I pressed my mouth against Tula's. Her parted lips were pillowy soft against mine. She tasted like bubble gum and sunshine, sweet and warm. I forced myself to keep the kiss soft and sweet, savoring the taste of her. What I wanted, though, was to attack her mouth like a starving man sitting down for a meal. I was definitely a starving man, but I was only hungry for her.

I deepened the kiss, and Tula melted in my arms. Her whole body relaxed, and her arms wrapped around me, weaving her fingers into the hair at the nape of my neck. She moaned as she did, and I returned the sound. She pushed onto the balls of her feet in a failed effort to make herself taller. She projected an emotion I could not put my finger on, and it swallowed our energy. There was something both beautiful and anxious about it. And she did not, for that one moment, try to hide anything. Everything was perfect about the moment. About Tula. About us.

As much as I thought slow and sweet was the right approach for her, Tula's response quickly proved me wrong. Had I known her reaction, I would have done it the day we met. The kiss grew more intense, and as it did, it conveyed an unexpected desperation. She was always in such perfect control that her response of abandonment of restraint surprised me. Her arms slid down my shoulders and onto my arms, only leaving my body long enough to relocate to my back. They continued past my waist until her delicate hands slipped into the back pocket of my jeans and grabbed ahold of my ass. It was the hottest thing a woman had ever done to me in public. Passion dripped from her pores as it had been building inside of her for God only knows how long. The heat from her radiated everywhere our skin touched. The smell of gunpowder from the fireworks invaded my senses, and I felt as though she and I were smoldering.

I needed her, and at that moment, there was no doubt in my mind that she needed me, too. I slid my hand from her face around to the back of her neck and pulled her face and body in closer to mine until we were pressed against one another.

That's when I suddenly became aware of an odd quietness around us. When I opened my eyes, I was distracted by Tula's beautiful face, flawless skin, and her full lips still on mine. Then I remembered why I'd opened my eyes. The fireworks had not only ended, but every person from the restaurant on the outdoor deck was staring at us.

Tula seemed to remember we weren't alone as well and pulled her hands out of my pockets and pushed away from me with the force of a snapping rubber band. When she looked around and saw everyone's eyes on us, her face turned beet red.

She lowered her beautiful face and said, "Maybe I will go home. I shouldn't have come in tonight."

Tula walked back to the office, only to reappear moments later, having removed her apron and grabbed her bag. Silently, she made her way to the front door, not making contact with anyone but keeping her head down instead.

I wasn't sure if the kiss had been a glorious success or a complete disaster, but I was leaning toward success with an abrupt ending. I learned something, though. When Tula said "This is a bad idea" just before we had a moment together, she was trying to talk herself out of letting her guard down. And failing. For now, the walls she had built to protect her heart were back in place. But if I got her to lower them once, even if for only a minute, I could get her to do it again.

Chapter Twenty

Tula

I SAT ON THE EDGE of the bed, rubbing George's ears, and thought about that kiss. The teenagers down the street were still setting off firecrackers and occasional larger fireworks punctuated the sounds of the evening. I jumped every time I heard them, and George would try to calm me with a slobbery dog kiss.

I wasn't sure which bothered me more that night, the noise from the fireworks or the way my stomach did somersaults when Paul put his arms around me.

I flopped back onto the bed, reliving the evening in my head. As I did, George walked across the mattress to the foot of the bed, sat for a moment, and then hopped off to go sleep on his bed. Apparently, his mattress was more comfortable than mine.

God, that kiss was electric. I could still feel the current flowing through my body when his lips connected to mine. Within seconds, I had forgotten where I was, what day of the week it was, that we were in public, or even my own name. I could not believe that I had put my hands on his ass in front of half of Jett's Landing. My aunt, uncle, sister, brother-in-law, and their kids were there as well. Oh, God! Lily would call all my sisters with a report on what she witnessed. What the hell was I thinking, letting Paul kiss me?

Getting entangled with Paul was a bad idea for so many reasons. I rolled over to the edge of the bed, pulled out a pad of sticky notes along with a pen from the bedside table drawer, and made a list.

Reasons NOT to get involved with Paul Reed

1. *Never get involved with people you work with.*

2. *My home is in Key West, not Jett's Landing.*

3. *I vowed a long time ago not to ever get into a serious relationship again.*

4. *All men lie.*

5. *He'll break my heart, just like the others did.*

After formulating this list, I made the obvious decision. I would not let myself get involved with Paul Reed. Because that's how it starts. That's how I end up heartbroken. I placed it on the nightstand, so I would see it every morning when I turned off my alarm. The next step was to convince Paul to stop this before it began. However, he had a different mindset.

Chapter Twenty-One

Tula

THE NEXT DAY, WHEN I showed up at The Oyster, I quietly entered the office to put my bag in the desk drawer. Glenn was back, and he and Paul were at their desks, sifting through paperwork. As Paul looked up, the phone rang, and Glenn answered it.

Paul walked over to where I was standing, put his hands on my waist, and gave me a sexy smile. "Hi. Did you sleep well?"

"No. I never sleep well on the Fourth of July. Too much noise," I said, trying to distance myself with curtness, not looking at him.

Before I could say more, Paul's lips were on mine, and I felt like a stick of butter left in the summer sun. I had to stop this before I got wrapped up with him.

Glenn loudly cleared his throat before I pulled my face away from his and looked into his gorgeous eyes.

"Paul, this has got to stop. No more kissing," I whispered so only he could hear me. "Especially when people are watching."

As I tilted my head toward Glenn, Paul said, "So, I can still kiss you when we're alone?"

"No."

I had expected him to release me and walk away, but the man pleaded his case instead.

"Why? You seemed to enjoy yourself last night. I know I did and that kiss just now did not disappoint."

"Because this is a bad idea. I don't do relationships anymore. They always end badly, and when they do, it's always heartbreaking. I'm not a summer fling kind of girl, either. And even if I did want to get involved with you, I live in Key West. You live here. Long-distance relationships don't work."

"Those are lame excuses." He bent his knees and leaned in so our foreheads touched. "You're going to have to do better than that."

"Paul, you don't know me. I've got some serious baggage from things that have happened in my life. Trust me when I say, you don't want any part of it." I grabbed his wrists and unwrapped his hands from my waist before turning to walk away. But his words brought me to an abrupt halt.

"You do realize that nowhere in all of your reasons why we shouldn't be together did you say you weren't attracted to me."

"I know," I said with a sigh and then walked out of the office and headed to the kitchen.

Chapter Twenty-Two

Paul

I LEFT TULA ALONE for a while, letting her start the food prep for the evening's patrons. I was sitting at my desk when Glenn threw a balled-up piece of paper at me and broke my trance when it hit me in the head. "Earth to Paul. Is anyone in there?"

"Yeah, yeah. What do you want?"

"What's the deal with you and Tula? I heard about last night and now this afternoon. Looks like you two are about to get something going."

"Yes. No. Maybe. I don't know. I think she just shot me down. Again."

"Are you losing your touch with the ladies? How sad."

I did not have to look over to know he had a stupid smirk on his face.

"No, it's just her. Something happened, I don't know what, but she does not let people get close. I mean, she's been here a little over a month and what do we know about her? She has a home in Key West. She is living with her aunt and uncle while she's here, drives a five-year-old Jeep, and has a well-trained dog named George. That's it."

Glenn took a minute to think. "You know what? You're right. None of us really know her. We should try to find out more about her. Maybe I'll ask her out. I might learn more about her that way."

Oh, hell no!

"Speaking of finding out more," I said, desperate to change the subject. "Have you talked to Peggy lately? Are there any new leads on Steven?"

"I talked to her about four days ago. The police have hit a dead end and have told her that until there's some new information that there is nothing else they can do."

"Poor girl. She's got to be freaking out. When you send in the payroll, make sure Steven's check is made out for the full amount, even though he didn't put in any hours. Peggy's still got bills and a new baby. She'll need the money."

"Yeah, let's plan on doing that through the end of the year, so she can get the shareholder payout, too. If Steven doesn't show back up by then, maybe we should think about buying her out."

With nothing else to say, I nodded, walked out of the office, and headed to the kitchen.

I stood in the doorway and watched Tula work. She had been a quick study. In only a month, she could manage most anything in the kitchen, act as a hostess, wait and clear tables, and she was decent behind the bar as well. Those things weren't what had me standing in the doorway, though.

I was watching her. I noticed her spectacular eyes and cute, petite figure the day we met, but I felt like, for the first time, I was really seeing her. The twinkle in her eyes, her beautiful smile with dimples that formed when she did, and the graceful way she moved. I wanted her so damn much. Not just in my bed, although there was no doubt in my mind that she would rock my world. I wanted her in my arms, my home, my world. The question was the same one since the day I met her, though. How?

"Need something?" she asked as she looked up at me.

Yes. You in my bed.

"Uh, no. Just wanted to see if you need some help with the pre-rush prep?"

"Sure. The red onions for the salads still need slicing."

Smiling, I walked to the sink. Tula hated slicing onions. Come to think of it, I had never seen her eat one. I washed my hands before heading to the cutting board and onions laid out on the prep table. It was going to be a long night of trying to focus on the restaurant and not Tula. I grabbed an onion and got to work.

Chapter Twenty-Three

Paul

I T HAD BEEN A great day. I mowed the lawn, took my boat out for a ride, and grilled a hamburger for lunch. When George smelled the food on the grill, he wandered over and I put an extra burger on. He went for a swim, played ball with me, and I shared my meal with the retriever. George was a good dog. Tula trained him well.

"Tula! Damn, I forgot to leave her the payroll checks." They were locked in my desk drawer. I grabbed my office keys and looked at the dog. "Come on George. Let's go for a walk."

George followed me to the restaurant but stopped before we reached the back door and lay on the cool grass under an old oak tree in front of The Haynie House Bed & Breakfast.

"All right, buddy, I'll see you in a few. The Oyster isn't exactly dog friendly, is it? We'll have to work on that."

When I opened the door to the restaurant, the aroma of baked apples wafted through the air, growing stronger as I walked through the kitchen door. Tula was pulling a pie out of the oven.

"Uh, we have desserts brought in Tula. What are you doing?" Tula jumped and almost dropped the pie. I felt guilty knowing my voice sounded harsher than I intended.

"The truck no showed this morning, so I whipped up some pies. Why don't we make our own, anyway?" She placed the pie on the counter.

"Because people can't bake anymore. It's a dying art."

Tula squinted, lowered the corners of her mouth, and wrinkled her brow at me. I could not tell if she was truly pissed at me or if she was joking around.

"We'll just see about that. Key lime, lemon meringue, apple, or banana cream?"

"What?"

She pulled a knife from the rack and waved it as she motioned with her hands. "What kind of pie? No, on second thought, you're tasting them all, Mr. People Can't Bake." She grabbed a dinner plate and placed a sliver of the apple pie and the others on the plate as she pulled them from the fridge. "Sit down."

Tula slammed the plate in front of me, and I followed her order.

Damn, she's cute when she's pissed.

When I did not pick up the fork quickly enough for her, she grabbed it and shoved a forkful of the banana cream pie into my mouth. I didn't finish the bite before I began talking.

"Mmm. This is good, really good."

She picked up the fork again and fed me a bite of the apple pie a little less forcefully this time. I waited for the next bite to arrive, but Tula stared at me.

Those eyes will be the death of me.

"Well?"

"Well, what?" Tula asked.

"More pie please."

She sat next to me and scooped up a bite of the lemon meringue pie. Tula fed me, allowing me to enjoy the slice of lemon heaven. I sighed, and the corners of her mouth turned upward.

"I think that's my favorite," I said.

"You haven't tasted the Key lime pie yet. It's infinitely better."

Then, she slowly fed me a forkful of the Key lime pie. The look in her eyes as she did was seductive and the slowness in the way she fed me sent my mind wandering to places I knew I'd probably never get to go with Tula. I imagined myself sitting in my dining room with Tula, having dinner, and then having her for dessert. As quickly as those thoughts entered my mind, she snapped me back to the present when she reached over and brushed a crumb from the crust that my beard caught. Her fingers lingered for a moment longer than necessary. However, her delicate touch was not holding my attention.

It was the extraordinary dessert that she fed me. Key lime pie was Tula's specialty. She knew it was good and smirked as she watched me eat. I closed my eyes and savored the bite before opening them.

"God, Tula, this, this is amazing! You really made this?"

"Yep. So, people don't know how to bake anymore?"

"I stand corrected," I said as I stood and smiled. "I'm firing the dessert company. You have a new job. Get to baking, Pie Queen." I gave Tula a quick, tender kiss before heading to the office to retrieve the paychecks.

I was never going to follow her no-kissing rule because they were even more fantastic than her pies. I just needed to get her on the same page. In the meantime, I would steal a kiss whenever I thought I could get away with it. And that time, I did.

When I grabbed the stack of envelopes from my locked desk drawer, I saw a piece of paper folded in half I hadn't noticed before. I picked it up and opened it. It was Dawson's handwriting. I blinked twice and then reread it to ensure I read it correctly.

Find Tula. She'll know.

I walked back to the kitchen with the note in my hand to find Tula wiping down the work surfaces. She was good about cleaning as she went.

"Tula, I just found this in the desk drawer I keep locked. What does it mean?" I handed her the paper and watched her as she read it.

She furrowed her brow, looking perplexed. "I don't know. Dawson obviously wanted you and no one else to find it. But I don't know what I'm supposed to know. Should we call the police?"

"Let's not yet. It could land suspicion on you. I mean, I know you weren't involved in his death, but the way he worded it—"

"Could look like he was pointing people to me as his killer," she said, finishing my sentence. "I wish I knew what it meant."

"I know. I wish I had found it sooner."

Chapter Twenty-Four

Tula

Paul's warm breath caressed my skin before his lips left a trail of kisses along the nape of my neck and continued down my spine as his hand slid over my skin. I sighed, closed my eyes, and slowly rolled my head back before turning in his arms to face him. When my eyes reopened, we were no longer on the beach in his backyard.

We were in a room I did not know, but the king-sized bed was beautiful and inviting. As we sat on the edge of the soft down mattress, he reached around the back of my neck and untied my bikini. He released the straps and the triangles covering my breasts fell forward. Paul took his time moving his hands to the ties around my back, but his lips were on mine like a scuba diver desperate for oxygen. I felt the weight of my eyelids close, and everything went dark.

When I opened my eyes, I did not know how long they were closed, but we were both naked, and Paul's face was inches from mine. His lagoon-blue eyes hypnotized me to the point of being paralyzed

"Tulip, you're mine. All mine. Do you understand? You belong to me, Tulip." His warm skin was pressed against my body, and I was consumed with the thought of the two of us passionately intertwined. "You belong to me," he whispered over and over again between kissing on my neck until the words morphed into the harsh sound of the alarm on my phone.

I opened my eyes as I reached out to turn off the alarm of my cell on the nightstand. I sat up, turned, and let my feet dangle off the twin bed. I was where I was supposed to be, in Aunt Cookie's house, in the bed in Dawson's room, with George snoring on the floor next to me.

"What? Now I'm dreaming about him? He's not *that* good of a kisser," I grumbled as I got out of bed and got ready for the day.

However, he was actually *that* good of a kisser. I was willing to bet he was *that* good at everything else, too. I gave myself a minute to consider all the things Paul could be good at before I shook the thought from my head.

Bad idea, Tula!

How many times would I have to tell myself that before I listened?

Chapter Twenty-Five

Paul

THE LOOK ON TULA'S face, when she stomped into the office, was a sign that something was not right. I went to work early to get some tax forms filled out. I knew she would be in to make the pies but had not expected the attitude that came with her arrival.

Had my finding the note from Dawson disturbed her that much?

She grabbed the mail on her desk, shuffling through it before shoving a large envelope from Key West into her bag before throwing it in the drawer of her desk and slamming it shut.

"What's got your panties in a bunch?" I asked with a smirk, hoping to improve her mood.

"You don't need to worry about my panties or anything else of mine for that matter!" She turned on her heel to head out of the room, but I caught her before she reached the door and gently held her by her arm, bringing her to me.

"Hey. Hold on a second. What's going on?"

"Nothing."

Tula's attitude wasn't like anything I had ever seen from her. She was usually even keeled, with a quiet voice, and displayed a calm air about her. Tula's voice was curt, and her forehead wrinkled from the pissed-off expression. This was different from the mocked anger over my statement about no one being able to bake. She was genuinely infuriated, and it wasn't over the note. Women had told me more than once that I was an asshole because I didn't always think before I spoke. Had I said something yesterday that pissed her off, or was I now paying for the kiss I stole?

I pulled her closer and lowered my face to hers. "Try again. It's obvious you're pissed at someone about something, and I have a feeling that someone is me."

She pulled away from me, not looking any happier. "Don't be conceited, Paul. Not everything is about you. If you want to do something productive, find Steven. I'm exhausted, and I need a fucking day off! Now, if you'll excuse me, I have work to do."

I watched her walk away, knowing not to push the subject. I would know what happened by the end of the day, though. I was certain of that.

Once Tula had the pies made and in the oven and her work area cleaned, I found her outside sitting at a table on the screened-in porch. She was on the phone, so I stayed just inside the door but was able to hear everything and see her as well.

"Yeah, I'm almost done, Gary. Just a few more things, and I'm calling it finished." She was faking a good mood. The pitch was too high to be sincere. "Once I'm done, I'll come up for a few days if I can find the time. This damn restaurant is sucking up every free moment I have. I'm sure you're right. It's exactly what I need. I need to get up to the city and have some fun."

I did not know who this guy was or what they were talking about, but I did not like the idea of another man knowing what she needed, especially since it eluded me. I knew one thing for certain; being in Jett's Landing and at The Oyster Bar was starting to take a toll on her.

She pulled the phone from her ear and looked at the screen before returning it to its original position.

"Gary, let me call you back. I'm getting a 911 text from my roommate in the Keys. No, that sounds good. Talk to you next week, then. If not sooner."

I continued to listen, stepping just out of her sight line as she disconnected and made her next call.

"What's going on, Callie?" Tula listened intensely, occasionally commenting with a yes or no.

"No, you did what needed to be done. As soon as I get off the phone, I'll send you the funds. The plumber had to be called. I hate that you had to handle this. Yes, I know you don't mind, but still, I'm not charging you rent this month. You've had to take on a lot of stuff that renters shouldn't have to deal with." Tula listened and replied. "No, my mood has nothing to do with you. I just need to get home."

A long silence hung on Tula's end before she spoke. "I dreamt about him last night. God, Callie, his eyes, and those lips. Paul's driving me crazy. And I swear if you suggest a one-and-done with him again, I'll kick you out of my house!"

From the best I could piece together, she was talking to her roommate in Key West. Tula had been dreaming about me. Shit, the dream pissed her off enough to where she wanted to go back to Florida.

Chapter Twenty-Six

Tula

BUSINESS SLOWED THE longer Steven was missing, especially after dark. It had been two weeks since anyone had seen him, and the rumors were starting to fly. Most of them involved Paul and Glenn. According to rumors, they were responsible for Dawson's death and Steven's disappearance. And after my uncle's certainty of Paul's involvement, I found myself dissecting the rumors, as they took on new meaning.

Glenn, Katy, and I lingered at the bar, waiting for more brave customers.

"Tula, what are you doing tomorrow night?" Glenn asked.

"Not coming here. It's my night off. And no, I won't pick up your shift."

"That's not why I asked. I'm going to check out the new restaurant over in Ophelia after the dinner rush here. Wanna come with me?"

"Check out the competition?" I shrugged. "I guess."

"Great," he said, grinning. "I'll pick you up at seven thirty."

Glenn walked away, and as he did, Katy elbowed my arm. "He's a fun time. I dated him for a while before he met his wife."

"Oh, this isn't a date. He's married."

"Separated. But it sounds like a date to me," she commented.

Paul was walking from the kitchen to the office and overheard the conversation. He looked at Katy, avoiding eye contact with me as he slowed his pace. I did not blame him. I was in a horrible mood the day before and was only in a slightly better mood now. I dreamt about him again the night before. It wasn't his fault that my emotions were in such turmoil. I knew I should apologize.

"Katy, who've you got a date with? I thought you were scheduled to work tomorrow night."

"Not me. Tula and Glenn are going out."

"It's not a date," I said, realizing I was going to be saying this a lot.

"Hmm, I see."

I wasn't sure what Paul saw, but I saw something in his eyes I'd never seen before.

Jealousy.

That's when I knew it was not the best time to apologize.

Chapter Twenty-Seven

Tula

"IT IS NOT A DATE, Aunt Cookie!"

"If you say so."

Cookie was teasing me, but I was in no mood for it. I had dreamt of Paul yet again, and it left me in a foul mood. There was no escaping the man. He was everywhere—work, the neighborhood, and now my dreams.

Cookie's phone had been ringing all afternoon. Rumors spread fast in Jett's Landing, especially those about who was seeing who. It spanned the range of "I hear Tula has a date with Glenn" to "I don't mean to pry, but I heard Tula and Glenn are expecting a baby."

"Maybe I should call and cancel. I'm not even that hungry."

"No, you should go. You look so lovely out of those work clothes, and I worry you don't get out enough." I looked down at my yellow polka-dotted sundress. It was flowy, with thick straps, and the hem landed just above the knee that I bought in the spring from a clothing shop near my house, in the kids' section. "You've been here for almost two months and, aside from the boating adventure with Paul, I've never seen you have fun. Your mother would not approve of this all work and no play philosophy of yours if she were alive."

Cookie was right. My mother would've hated the way I was living. She had been a free spirit in the truest sense of the word. It was only her love for my father that settled her down. She was well suited for military spouse life. Always ready to move at the drop of a hat. Always ready for a new adventure.

"I guess. But it's not a date."

However, the further into the night we got, the more I could see that, at least in Glenn's mind, this could be a date. The mindless chattering conversation, his hand laid across mine after dinner, the goofy smile on his face all screamed *date*.

As dinner ended, in an effort to make it clear, I shifted the conversation to work.

"What did you think of the monkfish? My shrimp were way over-breaded. I think we've got the perfect ratio of breading at The Oyster."

"Tula," Glenn said, sounding exasperated. "I don't want to talk about work tonight."

Oh, God. He really does think this is a date.

"Isn't that the whole point of checking out the competition?"

"That was just an excuse to get us out of the restaurant together."

He still had my hand trapped under his. I wiggled it until I managed to escape his grip.

"Glenn, I thought I made my intentions clear. This is not a date."

"But isn't it?"

"No. It most definitely is not."

"How disappointing for me," he said with a smirk.

I could tell he had no intention of giving up. I needed to make sure he understood this before we got back to Aunt

Cookie's house. Some men don't understand that no means no. Thank God Dad taught me how to defend myself. I hoped I wouldn't need to use those skills at the end of the night.

I needed to change the subject again.

"There is something I want to ask you about."

"Okay, ask away."

"I heard a rumor that the reason you go off missing for a few days at a time with your boat is because of a side job you have."

"What are people saying that I'm doing?"

His playful demeanor was gone, his expression serious.

"Running drugs. It's where I've seen you before. You dock in Key West."

He froze for a split second and then relaxed and smiled. "Tula, I think you overestimate my abilities as a boater. There's no way I would make that trip alone. And drugs? Between the Coast Guard and the DEA, I'm sure I'd get busted within a week if I tried."

As he spoke, he shifted his eyes from me to his empty plate. It was obvious he was lying. He had not kept eye contact and knew too much about whom he would need to look out for in order not to get caught. He avoided my question about being in Key West as well. I was going to have to tell Paul about this conversation as soon as humanly possible.

Chapter Twenty-Eight

Tula

I WAS POSITIVE FRIDAY was going to be a long day of awkwardness between Glenn and me. And I could not have been more right. The moment I walked in the door, the tension was thick and palpable. I slid my bag into Dawson's desk drawer, and when I did, I got my first glimpse at Glenn, who was sitting at his desk. The skin around his eye socket was a deep violet with yellow and green. The eye was not swollen shut but considerably larger than the other. And then there was his hand, wrapped in white gauze bandages, looking like it was done by someone in the medical field.

Neither of us spoke. We just stared at one another. This lasted for three or four minutes before Paul opened the door and sauntered into the office.

"So, how was y'all's date last night?" Paul asked with a smirk plastered across his arrogant expression.

It was the kind of look that made me want to smack him. Or maybe kiss him. Possibly both. I wasn't sure, but I knew that both were bad ideas.

I shot him a glare meant to wipe the silly look off his face. But he was looking at Glenn's face when I said, "It. Was. Not. A. Date."

"What happened to your face? And your hand?" Paul's mouth was slightly ajar, shocked at the damage. "I'm assuming you went to the emergency room."

"Yeah, five stitches in the hand. I've got to go see an ophthalmologist about the eye next week. They said I might have a detached retina, but we won't know for sure until the swelling goes down." Glenn looked over at me, expecting an apology.

However, I just raised my eyebrows and gave him a look that conveyed I thought he got what he deserved.

I could tell that Paul was processing all of the non-verbal cues while the angry tension overpowering the room intensified. He grabbed Glenn by the neck of his T-shirt, yanked him out of his chair, and pushed him against the file cabinet, cocking his fist, ready to punch. "What did you do to her? What did you do to my Tula?"

"Nothing! Calm down, man. Nothing happened."

Paul looked to me for confirmation. I stood, motionless, half in shock that Paul would consider punching out a guy who treated me badly. No man that was not related to me ever held me in such high regard and this was not the first time he had done so. I paused to collect my thoughts. "In the future, Glenn, ask permission before you start acting like you're part octopus with tentacle arms at the end of a night where the girl made it clear the evening wasn't a date. You're lucky I stopped you before you ended up in jail. Let him go, Paul."

He released him from his grip and Glenn fixed his shirt. "Dude, what is your problem? You need to get a grip. I'll be restocking the bar."

"We're not done talking about this!" Paul said, but Glenn was halfway out the door.

Paul and I stood staring at each other, now alone in the office.

There was so much I needed to tell Paul, but I did not know where to begin. I was stunned silent. Had I heard him right? *His* Tula? Had he really said the words *my Tula*? I was certain he had said it. I lingered on the thought even though where that went had bad idea tattooed all over it and would lead to nothing but heartbreak.

The room's tension shifted.

He stepped closer to me until we were inches apart. "What happened last night? Are you okay? I mean, he didn't . . ." He moved a loose piece of hair from my ponytail, gently tucking it behind my ear. The tips of his fingers lingered on my neck.

"No, I-I-I mean—I mean I'm okay."

Stuttering as I spoke was something I had never done until that moment.

"So, talk to me." Paul sat in his office chair, and I sat on his desk. He rolled the chair around until we were facing one another.

"The evening started fine. That restaurant won't last six months. The seafood was over-breaded and over-priced. Anyway, as dinner was wrapping up, I realized he *did* think it was a date. So, I made it clear that I wasn't interested. Then I broached the recent rumor about him."

"You did what? That was risky, Tula. He could have gone ballistic."

"He didn't. But what he did do was lie to me. It was obvious. And I am certain now that I've seen him in Key West. There's a couple I'm friends with that have me come out to their sailboat whenever they visit Key West. The last time I went to see them, I'm pretty sure Glenn was moored beside them."

"When was this?" he asked.

"A couple of weeks before Dawson died."

Paul looked at his desk calendar. "Glenn was gone for four or five days around that time. Okay, Glenn is now a priority. We can't risk the restaurant getting shut down because of him. But that still doesn't explain his black eye."

He put his hands on my outer thighs and rolled himself closer to me.

I let out a long sigh. As I did, Paul's expression hardened. "When we pulled into my aunt and uncle's driveway, Glenn killed the engine and, without saying a word, pressed his lips to mine. The next thing I knew, he was climbing over the gear shift and onto me with his hands all over my body, trying to pull my sundress up."

"Jesus." He stood and slid his hands up my body until they were at the small of my back. "I am so sorry."

"It's not your fault."

The thought of it all pushed adrenaline into my bloodstream and left my head pounding and my body trembling.

"Tell me the rest."

"I told him no twice and when he didn't listen, I punched him. He rolled off me, and I rolled out of his convertible onto the gravel driveway." He scanned my body until he saw my knees, which were exposed by my shorts, still pink and scratched up. He was seething. "I got up and ran into the house. When I opened the door, George ran out, barking his head off, and didn't stop running. He jumped into Glenn's car and bit his hand. He's never attacked anyone before. I had to go back out to the car and pull George away."

"Good dog! I thought I heard him barking last night." I knew Paul would like that part, and I was right. He smiled and nodded. "I'll have to grill him some hotdogs for lunch soon."

"I know it's kind of funny, but Paul, if Glenn presses charges, the county could have George put down."

"Won't happen. I'll make it clear to him that if he even threatens to do it that he will be facing attempted rape charges. George was simply protecting his owner."

His hands remained on the small of my back, and I leaned into him, placing my hands on his strong forearms.

"Paul, I'm sorry I've been so angry with you this week. I'm just trying to work through something. I didn't mean to take it out on you."

"I know. I hope you work through it soon." He moved one hand and used it to brush my cheek with the back of it. I was certain he knew exactly what I was trying to come to terms with. "Maybe we can talk about it then, okay?"

I longed for his lips on mine. I didn't mind the kiss we shared during the fireworks or even the day after. But this protective side of Paul drew a desire from me I hadn't felt in a long time, and even then, it wasn't nearly this acute.

He placed the palm of the same hand he used earlier against my cheek. I looked into his eyes as I leaned into his hand, hoping he would kiss me. This reaction terrified me. Then I saw everything he felt at that moment reflected in his blue eyes. A pit formed in my stomach, knowing this wouldn't end well for me.

What the hell am I thinking?

I would be heartbroken by the end of this if I didn't get control of myself. I physically shook the feelings out of my head, came to my senses, and hopped off the deck, so I could step away from him.

"I know I've said it multiple times before, but this is a bad idea. I should go check on the pie inventory anyway. It looks like it'll be a busy weekend." I turned and walked away.

I didn't need to turn to know Paul was watching my ass scurry down the hall. I could feel his eyes on me.

128

Chapter Twenty-Nine

Dawson's Killer

THE AUTHORITIES FOUND Bella's body next to The Stack, naked and beaten. They never released exactly what happened to her, but I knew every gruesome detail the police didn't reveal. The bruised neck from where I had choked her after I violently fucked her was an obvious detail the public was unaware of. She wasn't dead when we pulled her from the water. She was only unconscious when I dropped off Dawson and Glenn.

I didn't need to kill her. No one would believe the little whore if she claimed she'd been raped. She had slept with most of the football team in her freshman year of high school. It was the first time I was brutal during sex, but it wasn't the last. Bella whimpered and cried, begging me to stop, while I held her pinned to the deck of the boat, facedown. The power I had over her pushed adrenaline through my veins. She was the first of four girls I fucked and then killed. It was like a drug. I craved the high and beat the girls more violently each time.

After Bella's funeral, the guys and I made a pact never to speak of that night again. They didn't know the whole story, but they knew enough to cause the authorities to start asking questions. That should have been the end of it. And it was for over a dozen years until Dawson grew a conscience. He told me the guilt was eating at him. That he had written the whole thing out and mailed it to the only person he could trust. I killed him the night he told me that. He was found in the parking lot of The Oyster with his throat slit.

I was beginning to think that Glenn might talk. He had been doing a lot of drugs lately. I didn't care that he did. The problem was, he talked about everything when he was high, and I was worried he would tell someone about that night. I could not afford for that to happen, and he had been behaving too irresponsibly to trust him. I was going to have to kill him.

Chapter Thirty

Tula

I TOOK MY TIME as I strolled in the muggy morning air and made the short walk to The Oyster Bar. The fish factory had been cooking since early in the morning and the air reeked of the oily menhaden they solely caught and processed at the Jett's Landing location.

When I was young, my grandfather told me it was the smell of money. He had worked the fish boats, like his father, and his father before him. When the factory was cooking, it meant he'd been working and a paycheck was on its way.

George walked with me, and along the way, we talked about all of the things we were going to do when we got back to Key West. Well, I did the talking. George listened and wagged his tail in approval of the things he understood and liked.

I found it was better for me to make the pies in the morning before anyone arrived to work in the kitchen. I wasn't in anyone's way. I could take up as much space as I liked and use all the ovens. It also gave me time to think. The peace and quiet gave me time to contemplate things. Lately, it had been Dawson's note to Paul. *Find Tula. She'll know.*

What am I supposed to know?

As I came around the corner, George turned and headed back to Aunt Cookie's house after receiving a pat on the head. After watching George walk home, I turned and saw Glenn's convertible sitting alone in the parking lot. He had already turned on the neon Oyster Bar & Grill sign, even though we wouldn't be opening for hours.

"Odd," I said.

Glenn was never at the restaurant before noon—when he bothered to come in at all. His irresponsible behavior annoyed me, but after our non-date, everything he did annoyed me.

Just then, Shawncy's little red sports car rounded the bend and entered the parking lot. She hopped out with the boundless energy she always projected. While she walked over to me, I pulled my keys out of my bag.

"What's Glenn doing here?" Shawncy asked.

"I don't know and as long as he says out of my way, I don't care."

"Wow! That was really a bad date, huh?" I started to speak but Shawncy continued. "I know, I know. It wasn't a date."

I rolled my eyes. "Have you seen the news about the hurricane?"

"Yeah, looks like it's going to be pretty brutal. Are you going to have to go home to handle your house before the storm comes?"

"No. I talked to my roommate this morning. She seems to have it all under control. Hopefully, it will change direction and not hit the Keys."

When I reached for the door. It was unlocked. We always kept the doors locked when we weren't open to the public. Just one more irresponsible thing Glenn had done.

Shawncy closed the door behind us and locked it. Something didn't feel right. I couldn't put my finger on it, but everything about The Oyster felt off that morning. I gulped as we walked down the dark hall to the office to drop off our bags. I stopped halfway down the hall and flipped the light switch on the wall. Shawncy continued ahead of me as I turned toward the office, just in time to see her trip over Glenn. He was sprawled across the hallway's floor, face up, eyes open, with a meat cleaver in his throat.

Everything was coated in crimson. Walls, floors, clothes, everything. Shawncy managed not to fall when she tripped over the body but found her balance on the opposite side of Glenn from me. She leaned over as if she were about to touch the body.

"Don't touch anything!" I shrieked.

I don't know how long I stood there, staring at Glenn, but when I broke myself away from my trance, I pulled out my phone and dialed. The phone rang until voicemail picked up. I disconnected and dialed again.

"What?!" Paul shouted, his voice gruff and sleepy.

"It's Tula. I'm at The Oyster. Glenn's dead in the hall. Someone put a cleaver in his throat."

Chapter Thirty-One

Paul

"TULA, HANG UP the phone and call the police. I'm on my way."

She had to be terrified. Alone, at The Oyster, with a dead body. Her words were a splash of ice water on my face, leaving me instantly awake. I dressed in lightning speed and hopped in the truck. I could have walked, but I didn't want Tula to be alone for a second longer than necessary, and the truck was faster. It wasn't until I pulled into the parking lot did I realize Shawncy was there, too. It was the day for our liquor delivery.

When I walked in, Tula and Shawncy were sitting at the bar, their purses slung over a chair. I watched as Shawncy poured two shots of Patron and handed one to Tula. They downed the tequila, and Shawncy coughed a little, but Tula handled it as if she took a shot of water.

"Ladies, I'm assuming the police are on their way?" Tula slowly nodded but didn't turn to look at me.

It wasn't until I watched her put the shot glass on the counter that I realized her hands were trembling.

I walked over to where they sat, joined them, and took her hands into mine. "Everybody good?"

"I'll be better when that shot of tequila kicks in," Shawncy commented.

Tula let go of my hands and walked into the kitchen. She returned with the schedule that was taped on the back of the door. "Paul, we aren't opening tonight, are we?"

"No, of course not."

"Shawncy, can you call everyone scheduled for today? Tell them not to come in. If they ask why, tell them. Gossip mongers will have it spread all over the county by suppertime anyway."

Shawncy looked at me, and I nodded. Tula stared into nothingness. She was operating on autopilot, and I did not know what to do to support her. I let her continue but watched her closely. Tula handed Shawncy the schedule.

"Bring it back when you're done. I'll need to rework it for the week."

Her voice sounded hollow and flat.

I was about to ask her if she needed anything when there was a knock on the front door. Before I could stand, Tula was at the door, unlocking it. Police and coroners entered. The line seemed to go on forever. Detective Neil Weston requested the three of us stay at the bar as he took us one by one out to the dock seating for questioning. He was the same detective who handled Dawson's murder and Steven's disappearance, so I was familiar with him.

"Mr. Reed, that's all you witnessed today?" he asked after I told him everything I saw and what I had been doing over the last ten hours.

Most of it involved sleeping.

"Yes, like I said at the beginning, I think Tula was so freaked out about finding the body that she didn't know who to call." I looked through the window and saw her sitting at the bar, reconfiguring the week's work schedule. She was making it look easy.

"I'm having trouble buying that she didn't think to call 911 first."

"I don't know what to tell you. She was definitely in shock when I got here. What did she say when you asked her about it?"

"She said she didn't remember calling you, or the police. Just that you showed up and then so did we. We'll come back to that. Did you know about the altercation the two had not long before Glenn's death?"

"I saw the aftermath the next day. Wait a minute, do you think she did this? The man attacked her. She was just defending herself." My chest burned, and a bitter taste filled my mouth. "As for his hand, her dog got between them, trying to protect her."

"That's exactly what she said. I'm not worried about the dog. She said he had never done it before, but that no one had attacked her since she got him."

I didn't like the implication but decided to leave it until Tula and I could talk about it alone. There was no way Tula murdered Glenn. I knew it in my soul.

"What do you know about the rumors of late about Glenn?"

"Only that there might be some truth about them. Tula told me she remembered seeing him docked in Key West. Do you think this happened over a drug run?"

"Did you know he was running drugs? I've seen your record."

"I haven't touched anything, but the occasional beer, since rehab, and I never ran or sold drugs."

I would forever pay for that poor life decision. I didn't try to hide it, but I didn't advertise it either.

"Are you sure? People say you've been acting differently lately."

"I don't know what to tell you about that. You want a drug test? I'll do one right now if you want. I don't know for certain what he was up to. Only what the rumors flying around were."

"I don't need a drug test. The fact that you're quick to offer one up tells me all I need to know. You wouldn't risk losing the liquor license for your restaurant if you weren't certain you could pass it."

"You've got that right."

"Tell me more about Tula."

I didn't like that he kept going back to her.

"I don't really know Tula that well. She only arrived after Dawson's death."

"But you work together every day. And I was in the restaurant the night of the fireworks. Certainly, you must know some things about her."

"Not really. She's a very private person. I know she loves her dog, misses Key West, and is the hardest worker I've ever seen." I wasn't about to tell him about Dawson's cryptic note. That would be disastrous for her since she had no clue what it meant. I didn't want to fuel the detective's suspicions, so I kept talking about my general knowledge of her. "She was an Air Force brat growing up. I think her dad instilled a serious work ethic in her."

"Wait a minute. Yates. Is her father John Yates, The Colonel?" I nodded. "Holy shit! I served under him. Toughest CO I ever had. I knew he was from around here, but I didn't know his family was still here."

"She's the youngest of his girls."

"And he didn't kick your ass over the Fourth of July make-out session?"

"Nope. Hasn't said a word to me yet, but I haven't seen him since either."

"Hmm. I need to talk to him then. If Glenn really did try to rape her, there's a good chance The Colonel is the man who killed him."

Chapter Thirty-Two

Tula

"**G**OOD GOD, TULA. They are dropping like flies. Hurricane coming or not, you need to come home," Callie said, her voice brimming with concern.

"Easier said than done. I'm going to be needed more than ever at the restaurant."

"Are you listening to yourself? Three of the four original partners are either dead or missing. I don't care how blue his eyes are. Paul's either the killer, or he's next on the list. Either way, it doesn't bode well for you. He'll kill you or you'll die last. Come home now."

We argued for a few more minutes before Callie conceded, knowing I was going to stand my ground, but warned me to be careful. After we hung up, I opened my computer and worked.

I thought I had only been sitting for a few minutes but when I looked up, several hours had passed, and I wanted to keep writing, but I was stiff from the wooden chair at Dawson's desk. In addition to that, I was parched. I stretched as I rose and walked downstairs to the kitchen, letting my rigid muscles loosen. When I reached the doorway, the light was on, and Uncle Parker was sitting at the kitchen table, can in hand, and his bloated beer belly was hanging out from underneath his shirt.

"I didn't realize you were up," he said as he pushed a chair out from the table with his foot. "Join me. We haven't talked much lately."

"Interestingly enough, we haven't talked since the dock incident."

"Hey! I apologized for that."

"Only because Aunt Cookie made you."

I grabbed a Coke from the fridge and leaned against the sink.

"There's something we need to talk about, young lady."

"Oh, really? What's that?"

"You need to steer clear of Paul Reed."

"Uncle Parker, do you really think I'm going to take your advice after you called me a little bitch?"

"The man is dangerous," he said, ignoring my question but not denying he made the comment. "And now that Glenn's dead, I'm positive he killed Dawson, too."

"What? You're not sober enough for this conversation."

"I've seen the way he looks at you, too. He looks like he wants to devour you. Or worship you. Or both." Uncle Parker's speech slurred on *worship*.

"Paul did not murder anyone."

I knew this in my soul to be true.

"Dawson got into a fight with Paul the night before he died. They were on the phone, and I overheard part of it. Something about selling the restaurant and a land developer. I don't think Paul knew you would be left his part of The Oyster."

"But Paul loves the restaurant. He didn't want to sell it. That was Steven's idea."

"I only know what I heard. It would kill Cookie if anything happened to you. You're her favorite of the girls, you know. You need to go home to Key West. You'd be safer there. That man is dangerous. I heard Glenn had a black eye and a torn-up hand before he died. They must have been fighting a few days before the murder."

"Actually, that was me and George. Self-defense."

"Holy shit! You are tougher than you look, kid."

Chapter Thirty-Three

Dawson's Killer

I WAITED IN THE thicket at the edge of the cemetery. I could see everything from here, and no one would bother looking in this direction. There was nothing this way to see. As I waited, I thought about the night Bella died.

I wanted to drop Dawson and Glenn off so I could fuck her on the boat, in the bay. I didn't love Bella, but we were eighteen, and she was not only easy, but all the guys told me she was phenomenal to screw.

I was speeding to drop the guys off at the dock, and when I hit the sand bar, she went flying, hitting her head on the side of the boat in the process. Glenn pretty much went into shock and Dawson freaked out. I jumped from the boat, grabbed Bella, and pulled her back on board. She was dead. At least I thought she was.

Dawson helped me push the boat away from the sand bar, and I took the guys to the dock. Dawson wanted to stay and help, but I sent him off to get Glenn home but not before making them promise to never speak a word of this to anyone.

I shook the memory from my head as the hearse turned onto Cemetery Road and stopped in front of the freshly dug grave. Other cars followed and then scattered to park. All the usual suspects were there. Glenn's family, friends, and a bunch of people I had never seen. I saw Paul's truck park a decent distance away from the burial plot. He walked to the passenger's side, but the door opened before he reached it and Tula jumped out.

Shit, she's still here.

I was sure she would have headed home by now. I heard she was the one who found Glenn dead. I did not want it to go down that way, but he fought me. I reached up and gingerly touched my jaw. It took two days for the swelling to go down, enough for me to be able to eat anything solid. Glenn had a mean right hook.

I watched and listened as the service began. It appeared it would be a long one. Prayer after prayer was being offered up and the minister was long-winded.

Tula looked fuckable. She always did. The dress she wore did not reach her knees and was fitted. I could picture myself putting my hand on her knee and sliding it up her inner thigh. I forgot about listening to the service and stared at Tula as I palmed the front of my thin basketball shorts and let my imagination run wild.

My eyes were all over her body. When she looked up during the third prayer and turned her head in my direction, our eyes locked. In the blink of an eye, I turned my body out of sight and pushed my back against the rough bark of the tree I had been standing beside. It was then that I had an epiphany. Dawson mailed his confession to Tula. She was the only one he could trust. That's why he left her his part of the bar. It did not matter now, though. Even the possibility of her knowing what I did, along with spotting me, was too much.

She would be the next to die. I would enjoy this one the most. I'd make sure she cried and begged me to stop while I fucked her over and over again. I wanted to hear her scream before I killed her with my bare hands.

Chapter Thirty-Four

Tula

I T WAS UNUSUALLY COOL the day Glenn was buried. Summers in Northeastern Virginia tend to have highs in the upper nineties, but on that day, the breeze barely reached eighty. The days before a hurricane made landfall were usually humid and oppressively hot. This one seemed to be doing the opposite as it worked its way up the Atlantic seaboard, scheduled to make landfall along the Carolina coast. It had been a very strange summer where the weather was concerned.

Glenn's mother and father, along with his estranged wife, made the arrangements for the service. The funeral was held at the Episcopal Church in Barley Cove. His wife grew up in that church and knew everyone involved in it. My guess was that it made the arrangements simpler to manage.

I sat in a pew midway down the aisle and the large stained-glass window next to it displayed Jesus's crucifixion. I was staring at it when Paul sat next to me. I wasn't aware of his presence until he reached over and encased my hand in his. He had never held my hand before, and I liked it. And the fact that I liked it scared me.

I wished I was somewhere, anywhere other than Glenn's funeral. When the service began, I originally tried to focus on what the minister was saying and not the man next to me, holding my hand. However, listening to someone speak about the life of a man I found dead was unnerving, and in the end, Paul holding my hand turned out to be a welcome distraction.

After the burial, the church hosted a reception at their fellowship hall. The hall was generic, with white-painted cinderblock walls, fluorescent lighting, and linoleum flooring. The folding tables and chairs reminded me of a high school cafeteria—only the food here was much better. All the ladies in the community brought a dish, creating what seemed like an endless buffet of country cooking.

Dad and I were waiting in the buffet line when he tried to ease into a conversation. He asked how I liked being in Jett's Landing and if the restaurant was staying afloat financially with all that had happened before he got to the heart of the things that were really on his mind.

"Why didn't you tell me about your date with Glenn?" he asked.

I sighed.

"I knew nothing about it until the police called me to ask me some questions about Glenn's murder."

"It wasn't a date. We went to check out a new restaurant nearby, which, by the way, wasn't that great. At the end of the night, Glenn got a little out of hand, so I gave him a black eye and George bit his hand."

"I've always liked that dog." He smiled. "And you've always known how to take care of yourself."

"I learned from the best."

Dad made certain that all of his daughters were able to defend themselves should the need arise.

"So, what about Paul?"

I knew where this was going. It was one of the reasons I kept my relationships private.

"What about him?"

"Your sisters all called me about the fireworks."

"And?"

"You don't seem excited to have met a nice guy. Something's troubling you about him. Want to tell me about it?"

"No."

"I saw the two of you holding hands at the funeral."

"Yep."

"Is this turning into one of those conversations where all I get are one-word answers?"

"Possibly," I said with a small smile.

"Your mother used to tell me to *embrace what resonates within your soul* whenever I felt conflicted."

We took our full plates and sat at an empty table. I didn't know what to say about Dad's last comment, so I didn't say anything. We were silent while we ate, but every time I looked at my dad, he was staring at Paul, trying to figure him out.

Dad finished eating before I did and excused himself from the table, taking his trash and plate with him.

I sat quietly, picking at my food, while I thought about what my uncle said to me in the kitchen as people mingled, gossiped, and ate. I would never believe Paul could be responsible for this, even if some of the evidence pointed to him. Hell, some of the evidence pointed to me, and I knew I was innocent.

I looked at him across the room as he talked to Mr. and Mrs. Smith. They were an older couple who came in every Thursday and ordered the same thing. He always had the rockfish, and she always ordered the soft crab platter and substituted the fries for macaroni salad. Lately, they would share a slice of Key lime pie at the end of the meal.

I watched Paul as he spoke and gestured. I'm not certain what they were talking about, but my guess was that it was food related. He was wearing the same thing he wore to Dawson's funeral, a black suit, gray dress shirt, and no tie. He wore a black silk tie during the church service but removed it and unbuttoned the top two buttons of his dress shirt before the reception.

God help me. The man is hot in a suit.

I was probably the wrong person to judge Paul's character. Ever since he'd kissed me during the Fourth of July fireworks and the moment we shared the day after my dinner with Glenn, my opinion of him would change with my mood. I'd think about his kiss and feel warm and happy inside. Then I would remember why I swore off men in the first place and hated him for making me feel that way.

I was still contemplating my conflicting feelings for Paul when I heard my sister Rose say, "Staring at Mr. Tall, Blond, and Sexy again?" She had taken a seat next to me, and her elbowing my arm snapped me from my thoughtful trance.

When I looked around the table, only then did I realize that I was surrounded by my sisters, Rose, Lily, Magnolia, and Daisy. I knew this was not going to bode well for me, and I tried to flag my father over. He was taking his sweet time obviously not wanting to get mixed up in whatever was happening with his girls.

"Of course, she is," Magnolia, whom everyone called Maggie, commented confidently.

"I have no idea who you're talking about." I swallowed hard and hoped no one else noticed.

"Sure, you do," Daisy said. "We all saw you and Paul holding hands at the funeral."

We had held hands earlier that day. Not only at the service but at the burial as well. As we stood at the grave site, he reached over and took my hand, which was much more visible than when he held my hand during the church service. It meant something more than what my sisters had seen. At least, I thought it had. It was a pact of solidarity. It was only the two of us, and we would have to stick together if the restaurant were to survive—if *we* were to survive. But whether I was ready to admit it, it was more than that, too.

"Yeah, well . . ."

"Well, what?" Rose asked. "You're not getting any younger, Tulip. Look at him. He's a hot catch. Go for it. Maybe you'll get it right this time."

The last hot guy I ended up with left me devastated.

I'll never get it right. I'll never be enough.

"Go for what?"

I could feel the warmth of blush flood my face as the corners of my mouth turned down.

"You know, go get the guy. Settle down and pump out a few kids before you get too old. Don't you want to be happy?" Daisy, the closest in age to me, patted her massively expanding belly. At forty, she already had enough boys to start a basketball team but showed no signs of slowing anytime soon. "We all heard about the Fourth of July make-out session, too. So, don't even try to act like you're not interested."

Maggie put her two cents worth in concerning the Fourth of July next. "Can you blame her, Daisy? I mean, look at his ass. I'd have my hands all over it too if I got the chance. And I'm a married woman."

Why couldn't they leave me alone?

My sisters knew how to get under my skin. My face was ablaze, and I was certain it was deep crimson. I was embarrassed enough with my own behavior that night, and now my sisters were rubbing it in my face. They had to know that talking about it would upset and embarrass me even more.

Lily was the only one who had yet to comment. Since she witnessed the kiss firsthand, I fully expected some kind of snarky remark from her, but surprisingly, she remained silent. She only sat and watched the conversation unfold.

"Daisy, I'm not that old. As a matter of fact, I'm over a decade younger than anyone at this table. And what if that's not what I want? Not everyone needs a husband and family to be happy." I snapped back. "Did you ever think about that?"

"But you used to want it. Husband, home, kids, the whole enchilada," Rose said. "I'm sure you can find a keeper. You just have to make an effort."

She was the oldest of my sisters and with a sixteen-year age difference, I often felt like she treated me more like her child than a sibling. She was right, though. I wanted all of those things at one time. I thought about it for a second too long. All the dreams I had of family and children, all the time I invested in what I thought love was, and everything I sacrificed only to fail time and time again. The public humiliation that came with my last relationship failure was more than I could bear to risk again.

No one ever wants to keep me.

My chest tightened, and my breath became shallow. Paul, my sisters, my past, and knowing that the future would never look the way I dreamt was all too much. Tears welled in my eyes.

Just as Dad reached the table, I stood, grabbed my purse, and ran from the room as the first drop fell onto my cheek.

Chapter Thirty-Five

Paul

I WATCHED THE WHOLE thing unfold but could not hear their conversation. Lily was the only person at the table with Tula I recognized. What on earth had these women said to make her cry and flee the room? Tula was the strongest woman I'd ever met. I excused myself politely from the conversation Mr. Smith had struck up about the future of the restaurant and followed her out of the church.

Tula walked away from the fellowship hall and pushed the sunglasses from her head to her face. The sun was dropping toward the horizon, and while not overly hot, the sun shone straight into our eyes. She turned right and slowly walked down the gravel road, kicking stones as she went. After about what would have been a city block, Tula came to the end of the road and the start of the beach.

The tears that began flowing in the church had yet to cease. I had never seen her so sad. I wouldn't necessarily call Tula a happy, giggly girl, but seeing her with tear-stained cheeks was just wrong. She was usually stoic. Hell, she didn't even cry the day she found Glenn murdered or when she sliced her finger in the kitchen.

She slipped off her shoes, walked onto the beach, found a spot to sit in the sand, and let the emotion work its way out of her system. It was only once she felt close to done did she realize that I was sitting next to her with my arm around her, and she had leaned into my shoulder. She sniffled, sat up, took her sunglasses off, and wiped the tears away from her face with the back of her sandy hands, leaving a few grains on her cheeks.

"Wanna talk about it?"

"No, not really." She wiggled just enough that I knew it was time to loosen my grip, and I moved my hand down to the sand but stayed next to her.

The wall she'd built around herself was so damned frustrating.

"Wanna talk at all?"

Tula shook her head all the while staring out into the water.

"We'll just sit, then." I reached over and patted her hand but didn't bother moving mine when I was done.

And that's what we did. We sat with my hand over hers in the sand. We sat long enough to watch the sunset and the moonrise in the partially clouded sky. Tula, even in her current emotional state, was stunningly beautiful. She always was. The moon illuminated her beautiful strawberry-blonde-and-copper locks piled on top of her head, as well as her soft, bare shoulders peeking through her sleeveless black linen dress. She was honestly the most beautiful woman I had ever seen.

"What?"

It was only when she quietly said that single word did I realize that not only had Tula noticed I was staring, but her voice was filled with exhaustion. Ever since Tula had arrived in Jett's Landing her energy level had been on a downward slope. It was obvious and beginning to concern me.

"You sound tired." I stood and held out my hand to her. "Why don't I drive you home?"

Tula stood without accepting my help and a look of contemplation fell across her face.

"Paul, this is going to sound weird and may even make me sound a little crazy, but I saw someone at the funeral today, and they kind of looked like Steven. They were too far away for me to be certain, though."

"Where?"

"I glanced over at the group of trees that sits at the edge of the cemetery during one of the prayers. I thought I saw him by a tree, but then I blinked, and he was gone."

"Do you really think he's alive? No one's seen him in over six weeks."

"I have no clue. Maybe I'm just imagining things. As much as I don't like him, I hope he's found soon. The not knowing is horrible, and I barely know the man. I can't imagine what his family is going through. I mean, Shawney never talks about it, but it's got to be eating her alive. Regardless of the fact that he's a prick, Steven is still her brother." Tula yawned and took a few long blinks, as though she could fall asleep while standing in the sand. "Maybe I'm just delusional from lack of sleep."

She walked across the sand, stilettos in hand. I watched her float next to me, as though she wasn't walking but gliding on air when she reached out and took my hand into her free one. The action left me speechless and after sliding her shoes on when we left the sand, we silently continued our way back toward my truck, once again hand in hand. She had never instigated any sign of affection before, and it skyrocketed my desire for her.

Neither of us was in a rush. As we meandered back, Tula's voice, barely above a whisper, broke the silence.

"Any thoughts on who's killing our partners?"

"I don't know. Every theory I try playing out in my head doesn't work. What about you? Any clue who's doing it?" I asked.

"After Dawson's funeral, I honestly thought it had to be one of the partners, and I was really thinking it was Steven before he disappeared. He wanted to sell The Oyster so desperately, but since he's gone missing, I have no idea who's doing this."

"Did you ever consider the possibility that I'm responsible for all of it?" Paul asked.

"You are the only person I'm certain isn't involved."

"Really? I would have suspected me if I were you."

There was barely a pause in the conversation before Tula asked another question in an effort to steer away from the topic.

"Paul, what will happen to The Oyster now?"

"Do you mean Glenn's shares? His wife inherited them. She sent me a text yesterday wanting to meet. I'm pretty sure she wants us to buy her out."

"Good. Let me know what I need to do. However, what I really meant was will we reopen The Oyster?"

"Oh, we'll open tomorrow as usual. It will be fine. The bad weather from the remnants of the hurricane will probably make for a slow weekend but like I said, it'll be fine."

"You think anyone will show up? Two murders and a disappearance are not good for business. At the reception today, the old-timers were saying the place is cursed."

"I doubt that. But we'll be okay. We'll just keep moving forward."

I watched as Tula drifted deep into thought. I was pretty sure we had different ideas on what moving forward involved. To me, it meant keeping the restaurant afloat and figuring out a way to connect with Tula, but to her, it meant something different. I just wasn't sure what it was anymore.

"A dollar for your thoughts," I said, trying to keep the mood light.

"You keep saying that, and I'll have enough money to buy the Fisher House from you."

She could have the house. She could have everything I owned. I just wanted her in trade. I was not one hundred percent certain when I began to feel that way about her, but the idea of her being completely mine had been eating away at me for longer than I would admit. "Yeah, you just looked like you wanted to say something."

"Not the time, Paul."

I stopped walking and Tula followed suit. I faced her and lifted my free hand to her face. She did not lean into it this time. "Will we ever get another chance? I bet Glenn thought he'd get another chance to say and do all the things he wanted."

"Still . . ."

"Tula, what's on your mind?"

She deeply inhaled the salty night air before continuing.

"Every time I think things are settled enough for me to go back to Florida, something happens." I dropped my free hand from her face and put it in my pocket, knowing I wasn't going to like what I was about to hear but kept her hand tight in my other one. "I can't keep working twelve-hour days at The Oyster, writing my column for the paper in Florida, and expect my roommate to take care of my house. Something's gotta give. And soon."

"Wait a minute. You're still working for the newspaper, too? No wonder you're so damn tired all the time. Between the two jobs, what are you putting in? Sixteen, seventeen hours a day?"

"Something like that," she said just before another yawn escaped her lips.

When we reached my truck, I opened the passenger's side door. "Babe, let's get you home so you can get some rest."

Chapter Thirty-Six

Paul

TULA CLIMBED INTO the truck and fell asleep before I put the vehicle in drive. I really wanted to take her back to my house, lay her in a four-poster bed in one of the rooms I never used, and let her sleep for days. Actually, I wanted to put her in my bed and sleep next to her, but I needed to take everything one painfully slow step at a time. I thought about it constantly on the twenty-minute trip back to Jett's Landing. However, since she was living across the street from my house, and her family was no doubt there, I thought better of taking her home with me and made a left turn into her uncle's driveway.

I looked at Tula, who was asleep, relaxed, and more serene than I had ever seen her. There was no way I was waking that angel if I could help it. I pulled onto the grass to get as close to the front door as possible and parked.

I got out of the truck, walked over to the passenger's side, opened the door, and unbuckled her seat belt. When I scooped her up, she instinctively wrapped her arms around my neck, nuzzled her face into my chest, and settled in place with her soft cheek against my heart.

God, this feels good.

I carried her to the front door. When I reached it, The Colonel opened the screen door and quietly pointed upstairs before leading the way. As I struggled with how not to hit Tula's head or feet against the walls of the corridor that encased the narrow stairs, I noticed the living room was full of women.

The living room held a sofa, a couple of chairs, and a coffee table as well as the lamps, plants, and knickknacks that made a house a home. In the center was a large, round oriental rug in shades of pale blues and faded greens due to age and sun exposure.

The women occupied every last seat in the room, and a few were sitting on the rug. The only one I recognized was Lily. She and I were going to have a talk soon. I needed to know what happened that upset Tula. These were the same women that brought Tula to tears earlier in the day, and I felt every woman's gaze on me.

I followed The Colonel into a small bedroom, obviously Dawson's childhood room. He backed out of the way as I gently laid Tula across the twin-sized bed, careful not to wake her. I slipped her shoes off her tiny feet and placed them neatly next to the bed. When I took her watch from her wrist and set it on the nightstand, I saw a list with my name on it. I picked it up and quickly read it. It was a list of reminders of why she shouldn't get involved with me. I would not call them reasons, even though the title of the list referred to them as such. None were based on me specifically. It was odd. If it had said things like *Paul is an inconsiderate asshole*, that would have been one thing. However, they were all generic, and with the exception of geography and my name at the top, the strange list could have referred to anyone anywhere. It was the last one that stuck with me.

He'll break my heart, just like all the others.

She'd been burned by love and more than once if the wording on that list was correct. Those guys were idiots. What jackass in their right mind would give up a woman like Tula? I put the note back in its place and stared at her. So lovely. So peaceful. I noticed a few strands of hair had fallen into her face. I bent over, reached down, tucked them behind her ear, and brushed the back of my hand against her soft cheek.

"She's going to be a tough catch," The Colonel said, startling me as my focus was solely on the woman in front of me.

"Excuse me, sir?"

"Tulip. She's terrified of relationships. Something tells me that won't stop you from trying, though."

I stood and looked down at her once more. I wanted to stay there with her, but knew that wasn't going to happen, at least not tonight, and not in her uncle's house. I turned my attention to the man in the doorway. "I should go. I'm not exactly welcome here."

"Says who?"

"Mr. DeWitt."

"My brother-in-law's a jackass."

"He thinks I killed his son."

"Did you?"

"No, sir. The man saved my life. Dawson gave me a chance when most would not give me the time of day. I would have traded places to save him if I could've."

We stood in silence for a moment, thinking of Dawson As we did, George made his way into the room and climbed onto the bed next to Tula, resting his head on her pillow. She wrapped an arm around him, instantly turning him into a canine teddy bear.

"I guess I'll head out. I think I could use a beer."

"Want some company? Parker drank this place dry as soon as we got home from the reception, and I could use one myself."

I nodded and walked toward the door.

"Where is he, anyway? I half expected a repeat of the dock argument when I brought her in the house."

"He passed out about forty minutes ago. I heard about the dock incident, and I was not happy about it. Parker got an earful from me. I don't care if he remembers it or not."

"Same here. He can be falling down drunk if he wants but when he messes with Tula, he's crossed the line." The Colonel tilted his head to the side and narrowed his eyes.

He was trying to figure me out. It wasn't difficult. I wanted his daughter, but I didn't say that. I just quietly closed the bedroom door.

As we headed down the stairs, I could hear the cackling and gossiping of women. Had I not known better I would have sworn there were a brood of hens in the living room. When we reached the bottom, I saw them— "The Hens," as I would forever call them—all still there, all hovering.

I stopped short of the front door and turned to them. "You made my girl cry. Don't ever make my Tula cry again. Have I made myself clear?"

My deep voice silenced the room, but I could hear their sharp inhalations of shock. I didn't wait for a response. I walked out the front door and Tula's father followed. As I turned, I saw him raise his eyebrows and tilt his head at his daughters. Something told me the gesture meant that they should take me seriously.

I climbed into the driver's seat of the truck and Tula's dad joined me through the still-open passenger door. Tula's purse was still sitting on the seat.

"Hang on a second, Paul." The Colonel picked it up and took it into the house.

I heard the voices of The Hens begin, but they were quickly silenced by The Colonel. "Girls, leave Tulip alone. He likes her, and I like him. Don't give her a reason to bolt."

Chapter Thirty-Seven

Paul

ONCE THE COLONEL WAS back in the truck, I wasted no time reversing onto the driveway and the sound of crunching stones seemed exaggerated. When I reached Main Street, I steered the truck one hundred eighty degrees and turned onto the crushed shell path that led to my own home.

"You live in the Fisher House? I thought it was a bed-and-breakfast."

"I bought it a couple of years ago from the people who restored it. I was going to keep it as a bed-and-breakfast, but it was more work than I bargained for, and the restaurant was suffering for it. So, I closed it down. I like living here, though."

"You know, this is Tulip's dream home," he said as he opened the passenger's side door and got out. "If you can't get her to fall in love with you, you might be able to bribe her to stay by offering her the house." Tula's dad laughed, and I smiled.

Of course, I always smiled when I thought of Tula.

"Trust me, the thought has crossed my mind."

We entered the house and flipped on the occasional light switch until we reached the kitchen. The kitchen had been remodeled by the previous owners, and they had done an outstanding job. The quartz countertops and stainless-steel appliances looked inviting, and they had taken the area that was once reserved for a kitchen table and converted it into a space for a second island, designed to be a plating area when fixing meals for guests when it was a bed-and-breakfast. The previous summer, I had six custom chairs built, so it could be used as a breakfast bar.

I grabbed a couple of long-neck bottles from the fridge, and we walked to the back of the house and sat on the screened-in porch.

When I opened the beers, The Colonel retrieved two cigars from his shirt pocket. "Do you mind?"

"Not if the second one's for me." I smiled and The Colonel handed me the cigar.

They were Cubans. Really good Cubans. I didn't want to know how he had gotten his hands on them, but I knew if I were The Colonel, I would be saving them for a special occasion and wondered what justified their use. I would find out later that Cubans were the only cigars he smoked. Once they were lit, we sat, listening to the frogs croaking in the night air before I asked a question that had puzzled me ever since I met The Colonel.

"Can I ask you a question, sir?"

"You just did," he responded while chuckling. For a career military man, The Colonel had a jolly disposition. "What's on your mind, son?"

"Tula." She was always on my mind. "Why do you call her Tulip?"

"Because that's her name. Tulip Renée Yates. All of her sisters are named after flowers. Rose, Lily, Magnolia, Daisy, and Tulip. It was a thing with her mom. She used to say we were growing a garden of children together." I watched as he was obviously thinking of his late wife. I waited until he smiled before continuing my questions.

"And why doesn't she like it?"

"She told me that no one would take her seriously in the working world with a name like Tulip, so she altered it. I don't think she legally changed it, though."

"Why Tulip?"

I got the impression The Colonel did nothing without purpose.

The Colonel looked at me, and I could tell he was debating how much to tell me about the life of the amazing woman I had just carried upstairs and tucked into bed.

"Because tulips are beautiful but have a short life span. Tulip wasn't supposed to live, Paul. She was born at twenty-four weeks and weighed less than two pounds. The doctors told us she probably wouldn't live more than a couple of days. And even then, only if she survived the heart surgery she needed immediately after being born."

Her scar. That's where it came from.

"Wow! I had no idea. Is that why she's so tiny?"

"Yes. Her mother was five foot ten, and I'm about six-two. Her sisters are all pretty tall, too. She definitely should have been taller. It's also why she wears contacts. She's mostly blind without them."

I didn't know she wore contacts. I wondered what else I didn't know about her. We sat in silence before I finally got around to asking him the question he had to know was coming. I puffed the cigar and blew it out before speaking.

"What did those women say that made her so upset today?"

"Why do you ask?"

"She's just so tough," I replied. "I mean, she finds someone she knows with a meat cleaver in his throat and to the best of my knowledge, she didn't even scream."

"Out of curiosity, what did she do?"

"She had a shot of tequila, gave the police her statement, re-worked the next week's schedule, waited for the coroner to leave with the body, had another shot of tequila, and then cleaned up the mess."

"I guess you would see her as tough. And my little princess is. Any girl that can shoot tequila the way she does is usually a tough cookie. Just not with her sisters."

"Those hens are her sisters?" I paused and reflected. "I'm sorry. That was rude of me to say. They're your daughters as well."

The Colonel tried holding back laughter but found it impossible. He was still chuckling when he responded. "That they are, but hens are an excellent description of them. I will now forever have the vision of them with feathers, pecking around, and clucking whenever they are all together. Well, all but Tulip. She never quite fit in with them when she was growing up. I thought maybe it was because she's so much younger than them. When she was older, I realized she was different from them because she always was trying to prove herself."

"Prove what? And to whom?"

"Well, her sisters are the *who*, but I never figured out the *what* part."

I decided it was time to circumvent the conversation.

"So, what did they say? Because I don't ever wanna do that to her."

"They called her out for having feelings for you." Tulip's father took a long look at me and puffed at his cigar. "Son, you've got it bad for my daughter, don't you?"

The Colonel looked surprised when I nodded. I guess he hadn't expected me to admit my feelings for Tula. There was no point in hiding the truth.

"Well, then, you should probably know, you're not the first guy in the last few years who's tried to get close to her. They all failed."

I thought about what The Colonel said. I knew exactly how I felt about Tula, but was it possible she truly felt the same way? I thought maybe she did when I kissed her the night of the fireworks, but the guard she'd been trying to keep up since had made me wonder. And after Tula walked hand in hand with me on the beach earlier in the evening, I had no clue what the woman wanted from me. I didn't understand her reaction to her sisters, either.

"And calling her out on me is what made her cry?"

"She's never told you about her last relationship, has she?"

"No, sir."

Tula's dad let out a long sigh and looked down at his empty beer bottle. It reminded me of the way Tula sighed. "Do you mind if I have another beer? It's a hell of a story for a father to tell without one."

Chapter Thirty-Eight

The Colonel

PAUL STOOD AND walked into the house to fetch more beer. I sat back and wondered if I should tell him everything. It was Tulip's tale to tell, but I liked the guy. Paul was polite, hardworking, and worshipped my daughter the way she should be. That was evident from the moment he carried her into the house earlier. He needed to know what he was up against if he was going to even have a snowball's chance in hell of winning my little girl's heart. I was still deep in thought when Paul came back with a single beer and handed it to me.

"You're not having another?"

"No, sir. One a night's my limit. I had some substance problems a while back, so I limit myself to one a night. If I even have one at all."

"Very well."

And he was responsible, too. Past substance abuse? Well, no one's perfect, but this guy was still looking like a better match for my daughter all the time. Most men would be in no hurry to marry off their last daughter, but I wasn't getting any younger and wanted to know my little princess would be protected if anything happened to me. I knew the concept was old-fashioned, but I didn't care. I was old-fashioned.

"Did you know that Tulip used to be an editor for a big publishing house in New York City?"

"She lived in New York?"

"Bought an apartment with her boyfriend in Manhattan."

"Really?" Paul sounded surprised. "I don't think I would have ever pictured her as a New Yorker. She's usually scurrying around the restaurant in cut-off shorts and a concert T-shirt, making pies and looking every bit like the Key West beach girl. It's hard to imagine her as a hard-ass New York businesswoman dressed all in black."

"Yep, but she was. Eric, the boyfriend, was the up-and-coming plastic surgeon to the rich and famous. Now that guy was the definition of a jackass. I think it was all that money he grew up with." As soon as I said it, I wondered how Paul could afford the Fisher House, the restaurant, the new truck in the driveway, and the boat tied to the dock. Damn, the guy was loaded. I wondered if he grew up with money as well while I took a long swig of my drink, or if he was a self-made man. "Anyway, I wasn't too surprised when Tulip called me one Sunday morning and told me they were planning on getting married in six months. Now, I do okay, but nice weddings don't come cheap, so I was more than happy when she and Eric offered to pay for everything."

"I bet." Paul paused, and I could almost see the gears turning in his head. He knew more than I realized. Maybe more than he realized. She never spoke of the wedding as being hers. On the rare occasion she spoke about it, she referred to it simply as The Wedding. "Oh, God."

"The day of the wedding, you couldn't have imagined a more beautiful bride. She had to be the most beautiful of all my girls on their wedding day, although I'd never admit it to them. Walking her down the aisle was one of my proudest moments."

"Why do I have the feeling this is where things are about to go off the rails?" Paul asked.

"Halfway through the ceremony, Eric looked at her, stopped the minister, said he couldn't do it, and walked out of the church. He hailed a cab and went straight to the airport."

"Oh my God. Tulip must have been devastated."

I smiled. I don't think he realized it, but Paul had just called her Tulip. "She never let it show. She took a moment to compose herself, apologized, and requested everyone join her at the reception. Tulip said that she couldn't ask for more than to have her friends and family together in one place for the evening. Come to think of it, that was the first time I ever saw her do tequila shots."

"Wow." I could tell Paul was beginning to understand why she was so terrified of getting involved with him. It wasn't just him. It was anyone. "When did all of this happen? Was it about five years ago? It seems like everything in her world was impacted five years ago by something. The Jeep, George, the move to Key West, everything."

"Yep." I put out the end of my cigar and looked at Paul. "And if that kiss on the Fourth of July was half as much as I heard it was and Tulip was a willing participant, then you're the closest she's let a guy get since."

"Well, I guess that's something."

"Son, I'm about to give you a piece of advice. Take it. Don't take it. It's your call," I finished off the remnants of my beer. "Don't give up on my daughter if you truly want her. But proceed slowly. If you don't, she'll run, and you won't see her again. Ever."

Chapter Thirty-Nine

Tula

I WOKE UP THE NEXT morning when the sunlight broke through the blinds of the window in my room. I did not know how I had gotten there, but I was still wearing the dress I'd worn to the funeral, and George was hogging the bed. The last thing I remembered was climbing into Paul's truck.

I could hear people moving around downstairs and wondered what the ruckus was all about. I took a quick shower and changed into cut-off jean shorts and a baby doll T-shirt. When I reached the bottom of the stairs, I discovered chaos that resembled a New York City subway during the afternoon rush hour.

"Am I that difficult to live with?" I asked no one in particular.

My father stopped in front of me, chuckled, and kissed my forehead. "No, little princess. The hurricane turned yesterday. It's heading up the bay, so we're all going to head home before the weather gets bad."

My smile turned downward until my lower lip pouted. "Even you? I was hoping we'd have some time to catch up."

My dad put his hands on my shoulders, and when he looked into my eyes, I could tell he knew what I wanted to talk about. I was ready to have the conversation he unsuccessfully prompted after the funeral. He knew if we spoke now that my sisters would end up in the conversation, but it did not stop him from saying what was on his mind. "He loves you. Just let him."

I let out a short sigh before replying. "But Dad, what if—"

"Tulip, quit letting the past haunt you. It's time to move on with your life."

My father had always given me advice in smooth, loving tones. However, this had a bite to it, more like a stern Air Force officer's order.

I slowly lowered myself into one of the living room chairs.

There was no use for me to pack up and head home. I would be driving straight into the storm. While watching the chaos unfold, I saw Uncle Parker carrying boxes out to Cookie's car. His eyes were clear and bright. He was freshly showered and shaved, too. He was sober. Sober for the first time since I had arrived.

"You're leaving, too? Is it not safe to stay?"

"It probably is fine to be here, but Cookie gets nervous. We're going to go visit her college roommate in West Virginia. Cookie hasn't seen Samantha in ages. We're grabbing the important stuff, just in case."

Aunt Cookie called out from the next room, "Parker, I've got another box ready. Tula, honey, where are you going?"

"I think I'm just going to stay here, as long as you don't mind. I'll be needed at The Oyster after the storm passes."

Cookie rounded the corner and sat in the chair across from me. "Are you sure you want to do that? You'll be alone."

"I'll be fine. And I won't be alone. I've got George."

"And Paul's right across the street," Daisy commented in a sing-song voice.

"What?" I snapped at Daisy.

"Just ignore her, Tula," Maggie said. "Daisy needs to learn to keep her big fat mouth shut."

My pregnant sister pretended to ignore Maggie and continued. "Come on, Tula. Stormy night, probably no electricity, and a hot guy across the street. That's got to be the perfect recipe for the horizontal tango."

"Sounds more like a porn flick," Rose commented, giving Daisy an exasperated look.

"That works, too," Daisy said.

"Okay, I think that's enough of that," Dad finally commented.

"Paul and I don't have that kind of relationship."

"Are you sure he doesn't want *that* kind of relationship?" Daisy asked.

Cookie jumped into the discussion. "Okay. I agree with your dad. That's enough of that."

"Do you know how you got in your bed last night?" Daisy asked with a smile plastered on her face, ignoring Dad and Cookie's request.

She was always ignoring what others said and blaming it on 'pregnancy brain'. She had been pregnant so much over the last decade that I was certain it was part of her personality if it wasn't before. As soon as the words were out of her mouth, she stood and headed to the kitchen to get a bottle of water but quickly returned.

Rose took her seat.

"Paul carried you in from his truck, hauled you up the stairs, and tucked you into bed. Then he and Dad left. But not before Paul spat some venom at us for making you cry. Dad didn't come back until well after midnight."

I must have looked as confused as I felt.

"Look, I know we've all been teasing you, and I'm sorry if we upset you yesterday. But it's obvious something is happening between the two of you. You deserve to be happy." Rose paused and watched Daisy roll her eyes before continuing. "And Sister, he referred to you as not only *my girl*, but *my Tula* as well."

Rose was right. I did deserve to be happy, but she could not guarantee I would not get my heart broken. No one could do that. I chose not to comment on the remark about me being his.

It was time for me to go home to Key West.

Chapter Forty

Tula

"**D**AMMIT, DAD," I SAID out loud, even though I was alone at The Oyster.

I was pulling the last of the pies from the oven. Who knew they would become so popular? People who had never come in before were now showing up just for coffee and pie. Two nights before Glenn was murdered, a customer asked me if they could purchase a whole pie to take home.

The customers were going to be disappointed when I went back to Key West. Barbi had been helping me bake some lately and seemed to not only have a knack for it but enjoy doing it as well. I would talk to Paul about the possibility of her taking over the desserts and sharing my recipes with her.

Paul had to know I was going to leave soon. Labor Day was in less than a month. I stayed much longer than I planned, but I couldn't do this forever. I needed to go home. I was becoming too attached to my life in Jett's Landing. I was becoming too attached to Paul, and that wouldn't end well for me. Relationships never ended *happily ever after* for me. My mind wasn't on the ten pies I was putting the finishing touches on. It was on the words my father said to me. *He loves you. Just let him.*

I wanted to believe that Paul did not love me and the only thing he wanted to do to me was X-rated. That would be easier to deal with than if he had feelings for me. But other ideas ate away at those thoughts. I liked being near him. He always smiled when he saw me, and I felt cherished whenever he was around. And that insanely explosive kiss on Independence Day. I still thought about it. Hell, I even dreamt about it.

"No, no, no!" I listened to my own voice and shook my head. "No more thinking about him!" I wiped the last of the mess off the counter I made while baking.

"Thinking about who?"

Paul was in the doorway, leaning against the doorframe with his arms crossed on his chest. He wasn't dressed for work but was wearing khaki shorts and a light blue Polo shirt. I liked this look for him. I wasn't sure why, but it may have been the fact it was something other than jeans and a T-shirt.

I did not see him come in and jumped when I heard his voice. "Good God, Paul. You scared me."

The corners of his mouth turned down. "Sorry."

"It's okay." I leaned my head in the direction of the pies. "What do you think?"

He looked at the counter. I had made five Key lime pies, two chocolate chess pies, two lemon meringues, and one he didn't recognize. He walked over to the last one. "What's this one?"

"Something new. I'd like to get us to a point where we have a different pie each night of the week and Key lime every night. It would simplify things in the kitchen. Anyway, this is a peanut butter pie. It's a fluffy peanut butter filling with a layer of chocolate ganache over the top on a graham cracker crust. Want to try it?"

"Smart idea about having a pie of the day. It sounds good. But I'll have to pass on the new pie. Mild peanut allergy." I knew it couldn't be a serious allergy because we used peanuts and peanut oil in some of our recipes, but this probably wouldn't make the menu. I didn't like the idea of making something Paul couldn't eat.

"Something else, then?" I asked.

"You know I could live off your Key lime pies. And I might have to. The Oyster isn't going to open tonight. I don't think it's safe."

"Excuse me?"

"I've been trying to call you all morning. The phone at Parker and Cookie's has been busy. The phone here is going straight to the answering machine, and you haven't been answering your cell."

Tula patted her pockets and then shook her head. "Dammit. I must have left it on the charger at the house. It was chaos there this morning." I looked over at the pies. "What are we going to do with all of these? I thought the storm was at least one more day away."

"It sped up this morning. The upside to that is the wind shear will break the storm down and decrease its intensity. As for the pies, let's stick them all in the frig. Well, all but one of the Key limes. I think I might need it to ride out the hurricane."

Chapter Forty-One

Tula

AFTER SPENDING SOME time doing what we could to secure the restaurant, Paul and I walked toward our homes. Storm prep wasn't nearly as difficult as I expected it to be. We brought in everything that was outside and pulled the rolling aluminum shutters hidden above each window down and locked them in place. Normally, one of us would have struck up a conversation while we worked, but my mind was too full to engage.

The breeze was picking up, and dark clouds were visible in the distance. When we reached his house, he invited me in for a piece of the pie he had carried home.

"I hope you aren't offended, but I'm going to pass. There's something I need to do before the storm hits."

"Is there really something or are you avoiding me? You've been quieter than normal today."

"I think I need to go talk to my mom for a while. I know it sounds stupid to talk to a grave, but . . ."

I couldn't finish the sentence. Not a day went by that I did not think about her.

Immediately after Mom died, I spent a lot of time mad at her for leaving me and Dad. Logically, I knew the cancer was not her choice. However, it didn't change my feelings toward her. After a short amount of time, I pushed down those feelings as well as any other emotions I had concerning my mother. For years, I never spoke about her and the long, painful road she had taken, trying to beat the disease.

Paul reached out with his pie-free arm and gave me a hug.

I'm going to miss this. I'm going to miss him.

"It's not stupid. Knowing she's gone and still wanting to share your life with her is not stupid at all. Do you want some company?"

"Not today, but maybe some other time."

"Why? Are you going to talk about me?" He flashed me one of his gorgeous smiles.

"I'm sure you'll be part of the conversation." I gave him a small smile and continued walking down the sidewalk toward the cemetery.

It was only a five-minute walk to where Mom was buried. Halfway there, George spotted me while sitting under a giant maple tree and joined me.

When I reached my destination, I saw the fresh wildflowers by her headstone. Dad must have picked them earlier before leaving town. Until arriving for Dawson's funeral, I had not been there in over a decade. However, no one knew that every Mother's Day I had a dozen purple tulips delivered to her grave.

I sat next to Dad's flowers, and George licked my cheek before wandering back in the direction of the maple tree.

I placed a hand on the stone and traced her name and date of death with my finger. She died far too soon. I still needed her. Neither Aunt Cookie nor any of the women in my family were my mom.

"I know it's just a place, Mom, but I'm sorry I don't come here more often. It's just so hard. I guess you know why I'm here. I'm so scared to give my heart to someone again. He's perfect, but I don't think I can do it. The last thing you said to me was to be brave, but I'm not brave enough to give my heart to someone. Not again. Not ever again. I just need someone to tell me it's okay no matter what."

"It's going to be okay, no matter what. I promise."

The voice behind me sounded like Mom's, but I turned to find Lily looking down at me. I never realized how much she not only sounded but looked like our mother. Within a few seconds, she was sitting on the ground next to me with both of my hands in hers.

"That's what she'd say. You know it's true."

"Then why do I want to run away?" I whispered.

"When you've been burned one too many times, your brain learns not to let you stick your hand near the flame. But Mom was right. You've got to be brave."

"One too many times?" I asked, ignoring her advice.

"You don't think I know about the other times? Every single time a relationship ended; we all saw it. Rose, Maggie, Daisy, and I saw how it destroyed you. Okay, maybe not Daisy." Lily smiled. "Every time, you pushed the people that love you a little further away."

We sat in silence while I tried to figure out what to say to her. We were never really close, yet she read me like a book. "How did you know I was here?"

"Paul called and told me you were heading here. I only live five minutes away."

"Paul called you? Why?"

"Why do you think? I knew last night when he walked through the door to carry you up to bed that he—"

"Don't say it. If you do, I might start to believe it. I like the way things are now."

"I always forget how much you hate change. Did it ever occur to you that maybe change can be good?"

"When has it ever been good? When Mom died? When I had to change high schools three times in four years because of Dad's career, and it cost me an academic scholarship? When Carl, Sam, or Trevor dumped me? When Eric left me at the altar?"

"Trevor? I missed that one. What happened there?"

"He told me I was funny and brilliant, but he couldn't get past the fact I looked so young. You can't blame him. I was twenty and looked like I was fourteen."

"You should blame him. He knew what you looked like when he asked you out."

I never considered it. I wanted to kick myself for not reaching out to her when I needed someone to listen.

"It doesn't matter. Change isn't good."

"What about when you got George or moved to Key West? Weren't they good?"

"Yes, but they aren't men." I paused, debating on whether to tell Lily my plans. "I think after the storm passes, I'm going home to Key West."

"Damn, Paul was right. You really are getting ready to run."

"He said that?"

"When he called me, he was worried you are going to try to leave before the hurricane got here."

"I considered it while I was walking here, but the moment of impulsive insanity passed, and I came to my senses. What did you tell him?"

"Your address in Key West, in case you decided to run." She stood and gave me her hand until I was on my feet. "Look, I know we're not close. I blame myself for that. None of us girls were there for you after Mom died. We were all relieved when you decided not to go away to school but to commute from Langley Air Force Base to Old Dominion University so that Dad wouldn't be alone."

"I couldn't leave him. He was all I had left."

"Exactly, he shouldn't have been the only one you could turn to. You had four older sisters and none of us stepped up. I'm so sorry, Tulip."

"Don't apologize. You didn't kill Mom."

My words were clipped and a little harsher than usual. Tears formed in my eyes, and the weight of the memory of Mom's final days crushed my chest.

"You sound upset. Wait a minute. Are you still angry about Mom's death? The cancer wasn't her fault."

"You weren't there!" I stepped back as I screamed. Tears rolled down my hot cheeks, and every emotion I ever pushed down about Mom's death exploded to the surface. I barely recognized my own voice. It was as if another person had stepped into the conversation. "She gave up! She stopped treatment, refused to go to the hospital, and stopped fighting. I didn't realize it at the time, but I do now. I thought she was all strength and poise, but I was wrong. If she can give up, I can, too. No more relationships! No more men!"

After screaming at Lily, I was out of breath. As I stood there, chest heaving, still crying, she just stared at me. After a minute, she calmly said, "Are you done yet? Is all of that nonsense out of your system? You know none of it's true. She only stopped treatment when the doctors told her it wouldn't buy her more time. And her one thing was that she didn't want to die in a cold, sterile hospital. She didn't give up, her body did. So, following your logic, you don't get to give up on love. Not yet."

"Don't use that word," I snapped. "It never ends well."

Lily shook her head and looked at the sky. "Sometimes love does. It ended well for me. It looks like the storm's getting closer. Come on, I'll walk back to Aunt Cookie's with you. I parked there."

I wiped the tears from my face as we started walking, and I was still thinking about everything Lily said when she asked, "Are you sure you don't want to stay at our house instead?"

"Where would you put me? You've got seven people in a three-bedroom ranch house. And where would I put George? Your two girls are allergic to dogs."

"Good point."

"Thanks for asking, though. I appreciate it."

When we reached the door, there was a note taped to it.

> *Tulip,*
>
> *George is hanging out at my house. I'll keep him here until you pick him up so you don't have to worry about hunting him down.*
>
> *Paul*

She looked at me and opened her mouth to speak, but I cut her off. "Don't. Say. Anything."

"Can I repeat something that's already been said?"

"I guess," I said, having no clue what she was about to say.

Lily cupped her hands upon my cheeks, and her eyes bore into mine. She had the same olive eyes our mother gave only to the two of us. "He loves you, just let him."

I said my goodbyes to Lily, and after she pulled out of the driveway, the breeze that built over the course of the day quickly shifted into a stronger wind. I grabbed George's leash and headed across the street. I normally didn't leash my dog, but he hated storms, and I didn't want him to freak out and run off. The storm hadn't started yet, but it was coming. And soon. The sky was getting darker by the minute, and you could smell the rain in the air.

When I got to the Fisher House, Paul didn't answer the front door. I walked around back, and sure enough, Paul was on his dock. He was finishing up his storm prep on the Calliope. I watched the waves breaking against the shore and dock, creating a white foam from the greenish-blue pre-storm water.

George was supervising. My crazy dog was sitting, watching every move Paul made. When he saw me, George barked once, and Paul looked at me with a smile. I didn't smile back. He finished the knot he was working on and then joined me at the end of the dock.

"You got my note."

"I did. Thanks for wrangling George. You just made my day easier."

"No problem. Did you have a good visit with your mom?"

"You mean my visit with Lily?"

He gave me a small, sheepish grin. "Did I cross a line there?"

"Probably. Don't worry about it." I was certain my eyes were red and puffy from crying. I was a crier when I was young but learned to shove those emotions deep within me. At least I had until yesterday. I'd felt emotionally out of control ever since I walked out of the church. "We had a conversation that was a decade in the making."

"So, it ended well?"

"I suppose. She quoted Dad."

"Can I ask what she said?"

"You can, but I won't tell you. Not now at least."

"Fair enough." He moved a little closer until we were inches apart. He cupped my cheek, but I didn't lean in. I knew I needed to start putting distance between us, so I just stood there, still as a statue. He pressed his palm to my face to mimic the feeling. "Are you sure that you and George will be okay during the storm? You're welcome here."

"This isn't our first hurricane. We'll be fine."

"I'll be here if you need anything."

"I know, you always are."

What he didn't know was that he was right. I wasn't going to listen to my dad's advice this time. I was going back to Key West as soon as the weather improved. It wasn't time for me to run home to Florida. It was past time.

Chapter Forty-Two

Tula

GEORGE AND I WERE not home long when the first drops of rain fell. I sat on the bed in Dawson's room and stared at the open suitcase on the floor. Why did I have to convince myself to pack? I wanted to go home, but there was something holding me back. Was it my concern about my Aunt Cookie? The restaurant maybe? Maybe it was because things weren't resolved with Dawson's murder, Glenn's death, or Steven's disappearance. I refused to admit the real reason. While I thought, George watched me.

"Don't give me that look. We can't stay. I can't stay." I stood and pulled clothes, shoes, and notebooks from the drawers, packing them neatly.

I hadn't brought that much with me, so it didn't take long. While I packed, George slowly moved to the door before lying in the doorway watching me. He was doing his best to keep me from leaving, but I could step over him if I wanted. He stayed there for about five minutes before he gave a small bark.

"I mean it, George. We are leaving." He stood, letting out a huff, and padded out of the room.

I heard him go downstairs.

I left out the things I would need for the next couple of days on the dresser and wrote a note to leave for Aunt Cookie and Uncle Parker, thanking them for everything. I would be gone before they returned. When it was finished, I tucked it into my backpack. I stared at the blank paper on the desk for a long time before I picked up my pen.

Dear Paul,

I wish I was brave enough to give you everything you need, everything you want, everything you deserve.

But I can't be that girl for you.

I read what I had written over and over again. I did not know what else to write, but this was the right thing to do. I wasn't brave. Brave people didn't run away when they were scared. But if I was running away to keep from being brokenhearted; why did I feel like my heart was already shattered?

Before I could contemplate the answer, George reappeared and dropped an empty food bowl at my feet. I looked at my watch, and it was almost six. I had been at the desk for over an hour and had only written two sentences. I folded the paper in half and put it in my bag with the other note.

I'll finish it later. He deserves to know how great he is.

I picked up the bowl and talked to George as we made our way to the kitchen. "I didn't realize it was so late. You must be starving. I'll give you the fresh dog food in the refrigerator that Aunt Cookie bought you. That's your favorite."

I refilled his water bowl and filled his food bowl to the brim. I grabbed a piece of fried chicken from the fridge and picked at the thigh as I wandered into the dining room to look out the window.

The dining room windows were at the front of the house and the morning sun made it impossible to eat breakfast, even on special occasions, at the highly polished cherry table that could seat ten people. Twelve if you squeezed together tight. I recalled a memory of the last Christmas before Mom died when we ate dinner at my aunt and uncle's home. Laughter filled the house along with the scent of baked ham, sweet potato casserole, and chocolate cake.

I was pulled away from those pleasant thoughts when I heard the crack of a tree coming apart. Seconds later, I understood why it was so loud. It was in my aunt's kitchen and living room.

Chapter Forty-Three

Paul

SOMEWHERE CLOSE BY, the sounds of a cracking tree rang out over the volume of the radio station I was listening to in order to get storm updates. It was early in the storm for that kind of damage, and I wondered where it had gone down. As I walked to the window to investigate, my cell phone rang.

"Paul! The tree! George! I can't find him. I need help!"

The words were pushed out between sobs. I had my shoes on before I hung up the phone.

"I'm on my way."

When I opened the front door, my heart sank. The huge maple in the DeWitt's backyard lay across the house, with the top of the tree blocking the front door. As I ran across the street, the rain poured, and the wind pushed me around. Tula opened a window and knocked the screen out. When I reached it, she gave me her hand and helped pull me into the dining room. She was helpful, too. I didn't realize how strong she was until she gave Glenn the black eye

I had seen more tears fall from Tula's face in the last twenty-four hours than I had seen all summer. This time, she was not trying to hide them behind sunglasses or wipe them away.

"Are you okay?"

"George—"

"I know, and we'll find him. But are *you* okay?" She just stood, not moving, not talking. I did a quick scan of her, assessing her general health. She looked fine, but she was terrified. I pulled her into my arms and spoke softly into her ear. "Where was George when the tree went down?"

"He was in the kitchen having his dinner. But half of the kitchen is under the tree!" She burst into a fresh round of tears. She hiccupped as she called for him, but her voice came out like a whisper. "George! George!"

"George, bark!" I yelled and then listened intently. I thought I heard something. "George, again!"

"Woof," George replied, nearby. He could be heard even with the open roof and a tree laid across the house.

"George, again buddy." And he barked for me once more.

He was just on the other side of the tree. I released Tula from my arms and climbed over the massive trunk. Ring after ring in the exposed wood revealed the tree was well over a century old.

When I reached the other side, I was greeted with the slobbery kiss and wagging tail of a soaking wet dog.

"I've got him. George is fine."

I hoisted him up onto the tree trunk and climbed up next to him. I lowered George into Tula's arms. By the time I was back on the other side of the tree, Tula was sitting on the floor, back against the tree, holding her beloved pup, whispering to him, and crying.

The house, even in its destroyed state, blocked most of the wind, but we were all soaked. However, not one of us seemed to care. I gently placed my hand on Tula's shoulder.

"What do we need to get out of the house?"

"I need to get upstairs to Dawson's room. My clothes, keys, purse, phone, and laptop are all up there."

The way the tree fell, Dawson's room was still intact, but the stairs were partially blocked. Tula stood and told George to sit and stay before climbing around until she could access the stairs. Just a few short minutes later, she returned with a small suitcase, backpack, purse, tote bag, and a leash. There was no way she packed her belongings that quickly. She had already packed to go back to Florida. It was the only explanation.

"That's it?" I asked. "I thought there would be more."

"I only packed for a week when I came up for the funeral. I've got George and my laptop. They're the most important things. I'm sure there are things I've forgotten, but it doesn't matter. I have everything I truly need."

Chapter Forty-Four

Tula

IT HAD BEEN DECADES since I was inside the Fisher House. The last time I saw it, Kathy Mae Primlott lived there with her mom, dad, and six siblings. It was warm and cozy then but in desperate need of a massive renovation. Now, it was gorgeous. Whoever had done the work had amazing taste and every detail added something more to the house.

At the moment, George and I were soaked, dripping all over the parquet floors in the entranceway. Having been well taught by my mother, beach kids never traipsed through the house in dripping, sandy clothes. It wasn't unusual to strip down to our bathing suit or underwear when in this condition before proceeding to our rooms to shower and change. Paul had obviously been raised the same way. He left us by the door after stripping to his boxer briefs to get towels. George could not get much more naked, but I took his collar off and hung it on the key rack beside the front door. I pushed my flip-flops from my feet and peeled my jean shorts off. I was pulling my Duran Duran concert T-shirt over my head when I heard Paul walking back into the room.

"Another wet T-shirt?"

"Very funny," I commented as I threw the wet shirt onto the pile of soaked clothes.

"Damn! You're gorgeous." Paul blurted out, staring at me with wide-open eyes as the towels tumbled out of his hands.

George walked over, picked one up in his mouth, and delivered it to me.

I looked down, not having given much thought as to what was underneath my wet clothes. Pink lace with black trim bra and matching panties were the only things left on my body. And they weren't dry, either, making them nearly transparent.

I grabbed the towel and quickly wrapped it around myself. "Sorry. My sisters say I overcompensate for my lack of height and lack of curves by owning too many sexy underclothes."

"You have plenty of curves, and I say this on behalf of all straight men, feel free to continue overcompensating."

I shook my head and smiled, knowing my face was red. I grabbed a second towel and rubbed George dry, while Paul took our things to the laundry room. He was wearing gray sweatpants and nothing more. Between the storm and knowing Paul would be in a bedroom down the hall, looking all kinds of sexy, it was going to be a long night.

Chapter Forty-Five

Paul

I STRETCHED OUT ACROSS the bed, listening to the wind howl and the rain pound. It was still early, but Tula was exhausted from the day's events and headed to bed after we both ate the beef stir-fry I whipped up for dinner. I resisted the urge to check on Tula down the hall, knowing it would piss her off to think that I was worried she might be scared of the storm.

That wasn't the only reason I wanted to check on her. Yes, there was the obvious, I wanted her, but there was more. While we ate, I watched her. She was emotionally spent. I did not know what happened between her and her sister, but when she came to pick up George, her eyes were red and puffy. Whatever they talked about had pushed Tulip to the point of feeling hollowed out. You could see it in her movement and hear it in her voice. I knew her well enough to leave her alone.

"Why? After all these years, for Christ's sake, did I have to fall for a woman who would sooner have a root canal than get involved in a relationship?" I asked, knowing no one would answer. I found myself grumbling at my own question.

Just then, there was a light tapping at the door. "Paul? Are you awake?"

My heart raced as I jumped up. When I opened the door, I felt like I had just won the lottery.

Thank you, Jesus!

Tula stood in the doorway, her copper and strawberry locks cascading over her bare shoulders, barefoot, and wearing nothing more than a jade green silk nightie that ended mid-thigh. I took a long moment to enjoy the view before I spoke. "Is everything okay?"

"Something blew through one of the windows in my room. I cleaned up a little, but I think it's pointless until we can get the window covered."

"But you're okay?"

She nodded hesitantly.

"Good. Why don't you wait here? I'll get the window handled."

I climbed up the stairs after going down to the kitchen to fetch a piece of plywood that usually acted as a shelf in one of the pantries along with long screws and a cordless drill.

I stepped into the Amber Marie room. All the rooms were named after people historically connected to the Fisher House. The brass plaques next to each door explained the history. It was one of the things I loved about the place and had no intention of changing it, even as a private home. I carefully walked through the maze of glass and a single giant shell. The broken window was quickly sealed with wood and secured with several screws. I found the towels Tula used to mop up water and wiped off anything wet. I added the larger shards of glass I found to the pile Tula started. When I reached the shell, I picked it up to dry it off. That's when I saw the fresh blood on the edge of it. After examining the window and where the shell landed near the headboard of the bed, only one thing could be true. Tula had been hit in the head with the shell.

Chapter Forty-Six

Tula

I HEARD THE THUMPING of Paul's feet sprinting down the hall. The door swung open, and he found me sitting on the edge of his bed with a bloodstained washcloth pressed against my right temple. I watched and could almost see the panic rush through him. The question that raced through his head was mirrored in the expression on his face. He was worried the injury was serious.

"Paul, really, it's not as bad as it looks," I said, trying to reassure him and help him find a calmer state of being.

"Let me be the judge of that." He sat on the bed next to me and lifted the cloth from my head, examining my wound. He could tell I was right this time. It was a small laceration, but it bled profusely, as most head wounds do. It was nearly finished, though. "Stay here and lay down. I'll be right back."

Paul walked into his bathroom, and I followed his order, stretching out on his soft mattress. He returned with a small first-aid kit, and I watched him as he cleaned my wound and covered it with two small butterfly strips. He attended to me and then used a clean cloth to remove the blood still on my face. This was only the second time he'd taken care of me, but I almost wished I were clumsier so that he could do this more often. There was something very tender in his attention.

That was the moment I admitted to myself that I loved him, even if I would never completely trust him—or any man, for that matter. And I was going back to the Keys, no matter what was happening with the restaurant. Long-distance relationships never worked. Nevertheless, I wanted him. Even if it was for only one night, I needed him.

"Now, I guess we should figure out where to put you to bed. Maybe a room with fewer windows would be a good idea." Paul sat on the edge of the bed and stared at me still lying on his bed.

The thought of another room, any room that didn't contain Paul, left a void within me. I felt this void grow, bit by bit until it was more like a crevasse than a tiny hole.

Just one night. I can let myself have this. And then I'll leave.

Even then, I was lying to myself. And I was okay with the lie but was certain I would regret it later.

"Maybe," I said with a whisper that came out more vulnerable than sexy. It was the opposite of what I intended. "I could just stay here. With you."

I sat up slowly and slid along the edge of the bed until I was sitting next to him, our hips touching. He smelled of fresh soap and nothing more, causing the corners of my mouth to turn upward. I was not a fan of men's cologne and rarely wore perfume myself. I stared deep into his now stormy blue eyes until we were both nearly in a trance.

"Unless you don't want me to."

He leaned over and pressed his lips against mine softly, as though he feared breaking me. I straddled him and wrapped my arms around his neck, lifting myself a few inches in an attempt to balance out the large height difference. Paul gripped me firmly around the waist, pulling me closer to him. He released his mouth from mine and kissed my cheek before skirting the freshly placed bandages.

"My poor, sweet, Tulip." He moved his lips to my earlobe and worked their way down my neck. As he did, he whispered the same words between kisses over and over as if he were repeating a mantra. "My Tulip. Mine."

His words moved me in a way I had not anticipated. Had he really called me Tulip and not Tula? No man had ever referred to me as 'mine.' Not even my former fiancé. I was so overrun with emotion that I felt my eyes welling up with tears. Paul noticed my reaction and stopped.

"Tulip, babe, what is it?" he whispered. "What's wrong?"

I shook my head before speaking.

"Nothing." I finally smiled and watched the tension leave his shoulders when he realized the tears weren't from pain but joy.

He kissed a stray teardrop from my face and returned his salty lips to mine. As he did, he slid his arms down to the bottom edge of my nightgown and pulled it over my head. The moment my nightgown hit the floor, the whole house went dark. In the pitch-dark room, I couldn't see him well, so I pressed myself against his chest.

Paul put his lips to my ear. "Stay here."

He turned, laid me across the bed, and was gone. I'm not sure why, but I panicked in the darkness for a split second until I saw a lit match and watched as Paul used the flame to light an oil lamp on the opposite side of the room. He adjusted the wick so that the flame stayed low, allowing only a faint glow to spread across the room. As he walked back to me, I pulled back the sheets, and he joined me underneath them.

Paul pushed away a stray hair that had fallen in front of my face before kissing me. "Now," he said. "That's better. I need to see you."

The next few minutes were spent fumbling with each other's clothes. Paul's job was easy, as I was already down to only a pair of cream-colored, lacy boy shorts. However, I fought the knot on the drawstring of his sleep pants. It did not help that my hands were trembling. Determination finally overcame the obstacle, and I watched as he tossed his sweatpants across the room.

Paul paused. "You're nervous?"

"Umm, yes. No. I don't know. It's just been a really long time."

His lips were sliding along the side of my neck, making a path toward my shoulder. His beard tickled with the motion.

"How long?" he asked, his lips continuing to meander over my skin.

"Five years." I took a deep breath and closed my eyes.

"Oh, that's not good. Not good enough for my sweet Tulip." He returned to his slow path of kisses along my body.

My mind was racing, and my body tensed under him. This was the way it began. This was the start of my heart being broken, just like every other time.

Paul moved until we were face-to-face and cupped his hands along my jawline. I loved it when he did that and leaned the weight of my head into one of his hands. "What scares you about this? I can tell you're holding back."

"It's safer to hold back. Every time I get involved with someone, I get hurt. I can't let that happen again, Paul. I don't think I'd survive it. If you're not okay with that, we should probably stop right now."

"I'll take you any way you'll let me at this point. I've wanted you since the day we met," he said. "But you wanna get involved with me, don't ya?"

There was no way I was going to answer his question, even though we both knew the answer. I pressed my lips against his, and Paul's kiss melted me. He caressed my skin as his hands slid from my waist to my hips before he reached around and rested them on my ass. His touch was firm and reassuring. It was as if I had spent the last five years of my life waiting for him, for the moment we were in, for someone to want me the way he wanted me. I pressed my palms against his muscular chest, and when I slid my hand down his body, I found him ready for me. He probably had been for some time.

"Paul, do you have . . ."

Before I could finish the sentence, he reached over me and opened the bedside table's drawer. It only took him a second to rip open the foil wrapper. After he put it on, Paul paused as he looked at me. I had seen the same expression on the faces of the other men that had made their way into my bed, although there hadn't been many. I sat up and straddled him once again.

"You're not going to break me. I'm short and skinny, but trust me, I'm not fragile."

Confidence appeared in his smile, and he rolled over, laying me back on the bed as I kept my legs wrapped around him. And as Jett's Landing stood firm against the hurricane, the walls I had built around my heart collapsed. I wasn't sure if I would ever be able to rebuild them, but I didn't care. As we made love, my loneliness melted away and my life seemed whole for the first time in years, maybe ever. I wanted to live in that moment forever and prayed both the storm and the night would never end. I was afraid of what daylight might bring.

Chapter Forty-Seven

Paul

I WASN'T CERTAIN WHEN I drifted off to sleep. I held Tulip for a long time after we were done and watched as she smiled with quiet contentment and rested her cheek against my chest. But when I opened my eyes and turned over to where I expected her to be, the bed was empty.

I sat up and looked across the room to find her silhouette in the window seat watching the storm unfold over the bay. You could hear the waves breaking against the sand and beating on the dock. The wood was no doubt, being pushed beyond its breaking point. I knew I'd probably have to replace parts of the dock again. The last hurricane's damage required dock repairs two autumns ago as well.

George was on the window seat, lying across her legs with his head on her lap, and Tulip was rubbing his ears. I hadn't been awake when she let her goofball of a golden retriever in the bedroom. Not that I minded either way. I loved her dog. He didn't seem to be enjoying the storm as much as Tulip.

I had no idea what time it was, whether it was day or night, and could not have cared less. As long as the wind blew and the rain fell, Tulip was mine. I just didn't know how long after the storm that statement would be true. I was in no hurry to find out either.

She was wearing one of my Oyster Bar shirts. It covered her more thoroughly than her nightgown, and she looked just as sexy in it. I silently watched her stare out the window, her beautiful hair framing her face, and tried to imagine life without her. I could not. But I knew she would not stay forever either. She made it perfectly clear, on numerous occasions, that the Keys were her home and that being in Jett's Landing was temporary. I stared at her until she looked over at me.

"Did I wake you?" she asked.

"No, but you're awfully close to that window," I said. "It makes me nervous while the weather is still like this. I don't want anything else to hurt you."

"Paul, what are the odds of that happening again?"

"I know, I know. It's just the odds haven't been in my favor lately. Two of my best friends have died and a business partner is missing. I don't think I could bear it if anything—"

"Okay. I get it," she said as she stood.

"Are you hungry?"

"Maybe a little."

I could feel her eyes on me as I walked to the dresser and turn the flame up on the oil lamp. I pulled a pair of boxer briefs out of a drawer and threw them on before grabbing a flashlight out of the top drawer. I walked to Tulip, who looked up at me, and I kissed her until she was breathless.

"Why don't we go find something to eat and then we'll revisit that kiss?" The corners of her mouth turned upward, making mine do the same.

I took her hand as she and I headed down to the kitchen. George followed.

She should have known that what I was going in search of was Key lime pie and a glass of sweet tea. Even though the power was out, everything in the fridge was still cold. I fixed our drinks while she sliced the pie, and we sat at the breakfast bar and ate by candlelight. George was treated to a Milk-Bone and a bowl of water. As we ate, we talked about my friendship with Dawson.

"How much did Dawson tell you about me?"

"Not much. He never really told me much about any of you. I might have met the other two guys when I was a kid, but I'm not one hundred percent certain I did. I remember Dawson talking about them. As for you, all I know is that the two of you were roommates in college. That's about it."

"Well, after college, I went to law school. That's where I met Linda. We graduated, both found great jobs in Washington, DC, got married, and bought a brownstone in Georgetown. We were living the dream. It all fell apart when I made partner."

"What happened?"

"Drugs. I had experienced a little pharmaceutical fun in college. But with the money I was making after I made partner and the hours I was working, cocaine became a fun fix and kept me up and going when I was working late. Then I was using it in the mornings to up my energy and get out the door. Somewhere along the way, it became all-encompassing. I couldn't function without it."

When I looked at Tulip, she didn't appear shocked or disgusted, and I found it amazing. I had spent so much time feeling that way about myself that I always expected others to feel the same. She only looked inquisitive. "How does someone come back from an addiction like that?"

"It sounds like a cliché, but you have to hit rock bottom. A couple of times. For me, the first was when Linda left me. She gave me a choice. I could have the drugs or her, but not both. I tried to hide my drug use from her, but she found out and packed her bags. Then, about a month later, I woke up in a ditch with my sports car wrapped around a telephone pole and had no idea how I got there. I didn't even remember getting behind the wheel. I could have killed someone. Thank God I didn't. I checked into rehab later that day."

She reached across the table and put her hand on mine. "That must have been terrifying."

"Looking back, it was, but at the time, all I knew was that something had to change. Dawson calling me about starting a restaurant could not have happened at a more perfect moment. I had been out of rehab for about three weeks and needed something to pour my energy into. The law office hours were already tempting me to relapse."

"Paul, how was the law firm different? You work at least twelve hours a day at The Oyster, but I've never seen you strung out."

"Well, I've been clean since before we opened The Oyster. Truth, though? I hated being a lawyer. I thought it was what I wanted to do, but at the end of the day, I despised it. Owning the restaurant, on the other hand, is something I love. I can't explain why."

Tulip smiled. "It's your passion. I can relate to that. I love writing."

"You know, I looked up some of your work online. You're a damn good writer."

"Thanks."

"So, why are you writing for some small newspaper in the Keys? You're better than that."

"I won't be there forever. I have a long-term plan."

As soon as she said that, I knew what she was doing. It explained so much. The exhaustion. The light, visibly on in her room in the early hours of the morning when I looked out the window. The conversation I overheard, which I now understood was with an editor in New York.

"Is your novel almost done?" I asked.

"How did you know? The only person besides my agent and editor that knew was Dawson, and he swore he told no one. But to answer your question, yes, it's almost complete. I'm handling revisions my editor suggested. A publisher offered me a contract."

"I didn't know exactly, not until just a moment ago. I pieced together a few things. Is it the same publishing house you worked for when you lived in New York?"

"Okay." She pulled her hand away from mine, as though she had touched a hot frying pan. "Someone's been talking to you about me. Was it Lily?"

I shook my head.

"Then, who?"

"It was your dad."

Chapter Forty-Eight

Paul

"DON'T BE ANGRY with your dad, okay? He didn't think you would ever tell me the whole story, and he thought I should know why you are the way you are."

As soon as the words came out of my mouth, I winced. I was an asshole for being so tactless, even if it was the truth. There was no doubt Tulip was going to get defensive, and I braced myself for the fallout.

"What do you mean the way I am? What's wrong with the way I am?! You weren't complaining about *the way I am* when we were in bed earlier. That's for sure!"

She stood from the table and began to stomp away, but I intercepted her before she could get to the door. George also stood, padded his way to the door, and lay across the threshold. Tulip looked at him and grumbled.

"George, you're a traitor. No more treats for you."

I hooked an arm around her waist before looking down at George.

"Don't worry. I've got you covered. Treats are available on demand, my friend."

I watched as his tail thumped against the floor before I looked back to Tulip and pulled her tighter into me. Even in the candlelight, I could see her cheeks were flushed with anger. I cupped my hand on her cheek and waited until she rested the weight of her head on it. When she didn't, I gently pressed it against her cheek.

"As for you, you know you've built walls around yourself to keep people away, especially men. *That's* the way you are. Should I have found a kinder way to say it? Someway that was gentler? Yes. And I'm sorry for that. I don't know what I did to get you to let those walls down but know this; I don't want you to put them back up, and I'll do everything I can to help you keep those walls down. That includes not lying to you. So, when you ask me a question, I'm going to give you the truth, whether I think you're going to like it or not.

"Your dad loves you. He wants you to have what he and your mom had together. A love like that requires two people, all in, all the time. Not one person with walls built around her heart."

"And you think you're my person?"

"No. I know I am."

Tulip sharply inhaled and held her breath. Her expression was that of sheer terror. This was bad. I knew I should be taking things slowly, one step at a time, and I skipped a few steps when I answered her question. After what seemed like an eternity, she exhaled.

"What happens when I go home to the Keys?"

"I don't know," I said. "But we'll figure it out."

"Paul, I am going back to Florida. You understand that it's nonnegotiable, right? I have a life there, and I'd like to get back to it at some point."

"Tulip, that *some point* is soon, isn't it? When you went to get your belongings from Dawson's room earlier, it didn't take you nearly as long as it should have for you to collect your things. You were already packed, weren't you?"

She said nothing. She did not move either. She focused on some distant point far away from where we were. Tulip was still processing everything I said. The silence in the room was deadly. I was losing her.

I guided her back to the breakfast bar, and we both returned to our seats. I had to get her mind off what I said about being her person, so I segued into another subject. "How did you end up in Florida, anyway?"

"Dad was stationed in Florida for a while when I was a pre-teen, and I always liked it there. When Eric left me—" She paused. I knew that sentence should continue with the words *at the altar*. "Well, after he left, I knew I needed to make a change. I just wasn't certain what it was going to be. Then I got a postcard from Cuba with two words written on it in his handwriting: *I'm sorry*. I put our apartment on the market the next day and gave my notice at the publishing house."

"You did all of that with no plan? Talk about taking a leap of faith."

"Yep. I bought my Jeep and started driving south. Found George as a puppy at an animal shelter in Charleston. I figured I would drive until my puppy, and I found someplace we liked. When I ran out of road, we found a home."

"What's your life like there?"

"Simple, organized, controlled, stress-free. Pretty much the opposite of here."

"You've been gone a while. Do you miss Key West?"

"I miss the predictability of my day-to-day life, but I miss the people more. I don't miss the constant threat of hurricanes in the Summer and Fall. Like everywhere, Key West has its plusses and minuses." Then there was an awkward silence in the room weighing down the humid air. I knew she was about to drop a bomb on me. "Paul, I think it's time for you to buy my part of The Oyster from me."

It was my turn to take a deep breath and hide my panicked reaction. The Oyster was the only connection I had to keep her in my life. God knows she made it clear that she was not ready to commit to a relationship that moved her away from her home.

"I don't want it. Dawson gave it to you for a reason. If you really want to go back to Florida, go. I'll hire more staff and have Barbi take over making the pies, but I want you to keep your part of the place."

"That's not the way the place operates and you know it."

"Then we'll change how things work. If I buy your part of the restaurant, I'll never see you again. And that's not happening."

I watched Tulip as a huge yawn escaped her, and we sat in silence. It was obvious she was desperate to change the subject, and I had no idea where to take the conversation. After a few long minutes, she broke the silence.

"I'm tired of talking. Let's go back to bed, and we can discuss this more after the storm is over."

We started the walk back to my room, and I let her get ahead of me so I could watch her hips sway as she moved.

"You don't really want to go to sleep, do you?" I asked, hoping for the answer I wanted to hear.

Without slowing her stride, Tulip pulled my T-shirt off of her body, threw it over her shoulder, and it landed on my face. When I removed the shirt blocking my vision, I glimpsed her bare ass turning into my bedroom. "What do *you* think?" She giggled.

I had never heard her giggle before, and it was sexy as hell.

I prayed the storm would never end.

Chapter Forty-Nine

Tulip

I WOKE WITH A HEAVY weight across my hip and thigh. I pried an eye open, and it took me a second to remember where I was and how I had gotten there. I looked down and Paul's muscular arm was laying upon me with deadweight. I turned my head until I could see his face.

What was I thinking last night?

"This was such a bad idea. So, you get to be the next one that breaks my heart, huh?"

His eyes were still closed when he said, "Why do you think I'd do that to you? I love you."

At first, I thought he was talking in his sleep, so I said nothing. Then he opened his piercing blue eyes and focused intently on me, waiting for an answer. It was hard to say aloud, but I was going to be as honest with him as he had been with me earlier.

"It's always the ones that say they love me that leave me broken." I could not bear to look at him and focused my attention at the foot of the bed.

"Tulip, stop. Not all men are like that." His voice was loud and deep. "I know what you're doing. Brick by brick, those walls are going back up around you this morning. You're going to have to have some faith in me for this to work. I'm not Eric.

"When I say I love you, I mean it. When I tell you I'm not going to hurt you, I need you to believe me. I know it's hard for you, and I know why. I can't change your past, but I can prove myself every day to you. So, let me."

As he made his case, he sat up, scooped me up in his arms, and held me tight with my back pressed against his chest.

"I want to. I just don't know how." I placed my arms on his, holding him holding me.

My hands shook. The smart me would have pulled his arms off me, gotten up, and locked myself in a different room with George until the storm passed. But I couldn't. I did not want to. Not anymore.

"Talk to me, Tulip. I know why you're scared. Tell me how to help you."

"You don't know why I'm scared. And why do you keep calling me Tulip?"

"Do I? I like your name. It's you. Soft, beautiful, and fresh when most of the Spring flowers haven't bloomed."

"Oh my God," I said, smiling. "You sound like my father."

"That's quite a compliment. Your dad is a great man. But you're trying to change the subject, Gorgeous. Your hands are shaking. You're scared. Why? Did Eric break you that bad?"

"It wasn't just him, Paul. It's every man I ever dated. Every man I've ever thought I loved. They all destroyed me in one way or another and then left. Eric is the only one the family knows about. And the only reason they know about it is that it happened in public. He's the heartbreak that pushed me to go to therapy. I really believe I won't survive another one. And now you're asking me to trust you. How do I do that?"

"You already do. You're just too scared to admit it. Yesterday, when the house was literally falling down around you, who did you call? Me. Why? Because you trusted me enough to know I would make sure you and George were safe. You have the trust. You've trusted me for longer than you realize. When you found Glenn's body, you called me. Because you trusted me and knew I would be there for you. Hell, you've trusted me from the start whether you'd admit it or not. The night you asked me to make sure you were never alone with Steven. You didn't know me then, but you trusted me to protect you. And don't think I took that compliment lightly because I didn't. You have the trust. Now it's time to let go of the fear."

I pressed my arms harder into his, and he squeezed me a little tighter as he kissed the top of my head.

Maybe he, my father, and my sisters were right.

Maybe it was time to let go of the past.

Maybe it was time to stop running.

Maybe it was time to be brave.

Chapter Fifty

Tulip

W E STOOD IN FRONT of the building, staring. There was nothing else to do. No amount of plywood was going to fix this. Every window in The Oyster Bar & Grill was gone, even though they were supposed to be hurricane-proof. Half of the roof was gone, too. Tables and chairs were scattered about, and I was certain a bunch were missing. The entire patio and the dock had been swept away in the storm. I was no expert but was certain the restaurant would need to be leveled and rebuilt from scratch.

It wasn't the only building that would need to be leveled. When Paul and I walked out of the front door of his house, we saw Cookie and Parker's house for the first time since we climbed out of the window during the storm. More damage occurred overnight as the storm battered it. In addition to the tree lying on top of the house, a section of the roof was gone, and the exterior wall that was once part of the dining room now leaned against the stairwell.

My intention was to call my aunt and uncle and break the news to them as gently as possible. However, my cell phone had no reception. Neither did Paul's. We agreed the cell phone tower probably fell in the wind.

I looked at Paul and knew the devastation of the restaurant was clouding his ability to think rationally.

"It's gone. It's all gone."

I wrapped my hands around his bicep, turning to reassure him. "We can rebuild it, Paul. We have insurance. It will be okay."

He sat on the curb of the parking lot with his head in his hands. I joined him, wrapping my arms around him, waiting for what he would say next. But no words came. After a few minutes, I stood.

"I'm going to go in and see what the kitchen looks like," I said.

"Don't bother."

I ignored Paul, leaving him on the curb. The building was probably dangerous, but I just wanted one look. I climbed over, under, and through things until I reached the kitchen door, half hanging on one hinge. I pushed it back to find the kitchen basically intact. Some pots and pans were gone as well as other utensils, but it wasn't in bad shape.

"Paul, you need to see this! Paul?"

There was a brief pause before I heard him throwing obstacles aside to get to the kitchen. He made his way through the door, without looking around, taking long strides straight to me. When he reached me, I was instantly engulfed in his arms.

"God, don't scare me like that! I thought you hurt yourself."

"I'm fine. I didn't mean to scare you. I'm sorry but Paul, honey, look around you. Tell me what you see."

He didn't look around. His eyes were glued to me. I never used a term of endearment with him. I only ever called him Paul. It wasn't lost on me that he was aware calling him honey was a sign something had shifted within me. His eyes said everything without uttering a single word. He was thinking that maybe I wouldn't run. Maybe I'd stay.

"Look around," I whispered to him. And he did.

"Our kitchen." It took him a few seconds to realize the most expensive part of the building was still intact. "Our kitchen! It's still here!"

Paul looked like a kid on Christmas morning. He opened cabinet doors and peeked his head inside the storage room. I watched as he walked to the back of the kitchen where the walk-in freezers and refrigerators were housed. I followed as he opened the freezer door. The cold air pushed against my skin. After a check of the contents, he quickly closed the door. Paul turned and looked at me.

"It's all still partially frozen, but it won't stay that way for long."

"So, what do we do with all this food?" I asked and then had a thought. "Do you have a grill at Fisher House?"

"Actually, I have two."

"There's one at Aunt Cookie's house, too. I mean, if it survived the tree. Are you thinking what I'm thinking?"

"Tulip, cooking the food doesn't solve the problem. Once it's cooked, we still can't store it without refrigeration and that can't happen until the power is back on."

"It solves it if you're going to have a block party," I said, allowing the smile on my face to grow.

Chapter Fifty-One

Paul

"THAT WAS FUN," Tula said casually as we started our walk back to Fisher House in the dark. The flashlight in my hand cast long shadows from the objects in front of us. I smiled and shook my head.

"We just gave away over a couple of grand in food. The restaurant is totaled, and you managed to find the fun in it. You are one of a kind, babe."

"How could it not be fun? It turned into a seriously good block party and none of the food went to waste. The teenagers that live in one of the newer homes somehow made music possible and even grumpy old Mrs. Lewellyn showed up and enjoyed herself."

We continued the short walk down the road. My arm was around Tulip, holding her tight against me. The storm was over, and the restaurant was pretty much a total loss. I was about to lose her. I knew she missed her home in the Keys and now she could return. But there had been a moment when we were standing in the remains of the restaurant when I thought she might have changed her mind. I prayed to God that I was right.

The streetlights were still out, but the men at dinner who owned chainsaws had gotten together and removed an oak tree from the middle of Main Street. Debris was still scattered about the street and lawns, but nothing that wasn't manageable, except Cookie and Parker's house, The Oyster, and the other businesses at the water's edge of town.

There was an uncomfortable silence between the two of us. Eventually, Tula couldn't stand the tension and spoke up.

"A dollar for your thoughts," she said, forcing a smile.

"That's my line," I said, then paused before addressing the proverbial elephant in the room. "I guess you're off the hook. There's no reason for you to stay in Jett's Landing."

Tula stepped in front of me and turned until we were only inches from one another, even though it was so dark I could barely see her. "No reason?"

Her voice was quieter and cracked when she spoke.

"During the hurricane, you said—"

"Forget what I said during the stupid storm. I knew I was lying to myself when I said those things."

"So, I have that effect on you, huh?" I wrapped my arms around her waist and pulled her hips into me as I smiled down at her.

She was mine. And I would never let her go.

"It's not just you, Paul." She put her arms around me, pulled herself tight against me, and I could feel the heat radiate from her body. "It's this town. The people here mean something to each other and to me, too. I don't think I realized that until I saw them all in one place tonight. And now, I'm not sure I want to give that up. I don't want to give you up either. I think . . . I think I might be in love with you."

I leaned over to her and whispered in her ear, "That was hard for you to admit, wasn't it?"

"You understand why, though? Right? It's not you, It's not even us, it's just me. I'm sure it will get easier for me to say, but it's going to take time. Can you live with that?"

I opened my mouth to tell her it was fine, and we had all the time in the world, but Tulip collapsed in my arms after squealing in pain, as though she had been electrocuted. A split second later, a shock ripped through my body before my knees buckled underneath me. I looked up just in time to see the baseball bat hit Tulip in the head and the face of the person attacking the two of us. Then the bat smacked the back of my head. The cracking noise was still echoing in my ears as everything went dark.

Chapter Fifty-Two

Paul

THE WATER SPLASHING OVER the side of the skiff landed on my face, causing me to stir as I became aware of my surroundings. I knew my hands were bound with a zip tie before I looked at them. Even in the dark, I knew exactly where we were. We were in the middle of Connelly's Creek.

"Tulip? Tula?"

"She's right here, next to me."

I knew the voice. Steven Faulkner wasn't dead or even missing. I went from confused to remembering who attacked us on Main Street. I moved toward the back of the skiff to be closer to Tula, but Steven lifted a gun with his free hand and pointed it at Tula's motionless body. "You move and she dies."

"Okay, okay. What the hell is going on, Steven? Is Tulip okay? We've been looking everywhere for you."

He answered no questions but continued to drive the skiff into the darkness. It was not until I saw a light along the shore did I understand where he was taking us. We were heading to The Stack.

"What the hell? Say something."

"I didn't want to kill Dawson, dude. But he knew too much. I'm pretty sure he told Tula, too. It was a long time ago, but it will ruin me if it gets out. I know she told you. You two, you're always talking. Always, giving each other those looks. It can't get out."

"What are you talking about?"

"How I killed Bella. And the things I did to her. I was so high that night. The drugs. The booze. Everything."

Steven did not have my attention. I watched Tulip's motionless body, trying to figure out a way to protect her from whatever was to come as Steven tried to justify a list of heinous things he had done.

Tulip stirred and opened her eyes. I continued watching her as she sat up, squeezing her eyes shut for a moment and wincing in pain. We made eye contact, and I could tell she was disoriented. She looked around and leaned over the edge of the tiny boat. For a moment, I thought she might jump. I hoped she would. She could swim, and it would not be that far to the shore and help. She was not coherent enough to understand the danger of remaining on the boat.

"Why are we on a boat? Why are my hands tied? How did we get here?" Tulip rapidly fired questions at me seemingly unaware Steven was on the boat with us.

She moved toward me, crawling across the skiff, and surprisingly, Steven did not stop her. When she reached me, I slid my arms over her head, wrapped her in the circle formed by my bound hands, and whispered in her ear. "Tulip, I know you're confused, babe. But listen. We're in danger. Steven killed Dawson. He killed Glenn, too. We need to get you out of here."

"He killed Dawson?!" Tula screamed.

Steven, who was securing the skiff at the only boat slip near The Stack, looked over at her, pulled the gun from his back, and pointed it in our direction. The light wasn't bright because the spotlights weren't turned on at The Stack that night. However, a single solar-powered lamppost near the slip made it clear that there was a gun pointed at us, and the light created long shadows of the three of us as we moved.

"Both of you. Out. Now!" Steven had the gun in one hand and a rope in the other. "It's time to go for a walk. No one will hear us around The Stack this time of night."

I stood to help my beautiful girl, but she sat on the boat, as if she had no intention of moving.

"Tulip, he has a gun. You need to get up."

"I can't." Tulip held her arms up to me, and I reached over, clumsily helping her rise. As I did, she whispered in my ear. Her voice was strong and steady. "I'm going to figure out a way for us to escape. He doesn't see me as a physical threat, but I'm sure he sees you as one."

"Okay," I said loudly, hoping Tulip understood I was in agreement, and Steven thought I was just helping her out of the boat. "Out you go."

When she stepped off the boat, I watched as she stared at The Stack towering overhead. Even though we couldn't see the top of it in the dim light of a singular lamp post, the recent repairs proved to have restored the extraordinary monument.

Normally, The Stack would be beautifully lit by giant solar-powered spotlights on all four sides of it. However, it was dark. It had not been lit the night before, either. I didn't know if this was intentional, in an effort to protect them during the hurricane, or if the storm had inflicted damage causing them to malfunction.

The lamp post gave off just enough light to see a few purse boats onshore across the lot where it met the water on the opposite side of the tiny peninsula. To the right was the original factory building. The factory was now located half a mile away from where we stood. Someone told me the building was being used as office space. Between the boats and the factory building there was a gravel parking lot. The Stack itself was surrounded by oyster shells and was landscaped with pampas grass. It looked nice and covered the spotlight equipment.

I watched as Tulip looked around as though she had been dropped on a different planet.

Damn, she's a good actress.

I followed her out of the boat, and with a wave of his gun, Steven guided us in the direction we were to move. Tulip continued to look dazed as we walked.

She stumbled and fell, landing on her hands and knees in the oyster shells that covered the ground around The Stack. She was so convincing that I couldn't tell if she intentionally fell or if it was truly an accident. My gut told me this was part of Tulip's plan. I just couldn't see where she was going with it.

When she tried to stand, Steven pushed her face-first into the ground with his foot, shoving her body completely into the shells below her. When she tried to get up a second time, he used his heel, which was covered in a steel-toed boot, to grind her face against the rough oyster shell exteriors, and she cried out. Anger welled up inside me. I was going to kill that man as soon as I got Tulip to safety.

"Paul, over there," Steven said, pointing his gun at me and then at the lamp post.

I walked in the direction I was told while trying to keep Tulip in my line of sight.

When we reached the light, Steven shot out the light fitting and bulb, showering glass over us. The electricity was still out in Jett's Landing, so, at first, I was confused that the light was on until I remembered it was solar-powered. All the outdoor lights at the factory had been converted a few years before the renovation of The Stack began.

Tulip disappeared into the darkness but not before I saw her stand and move away from us, deeper into the night. Steven had not seen her, as his back was to her, and his focus, as well as his gun, was pointed at me. "Sit. Back against the post. Hands over your head."

Steven put the gun in the waistband of his jeans and used the rope to secure my wrists to the pole before wrapping the rope tightly around my arms. After making a knot, he used the remaining rope to secure my torso to the post, adding more knots. I probably should have tried to get the gun from him before he tied me up, but I was worried that if I failed, he would shoot me and then find and hurt Tulip. I needed to stall him and buy her as much time as possible.

"Steven, it doesn't have to go down this way."

"Yeah, it does. The two of you know too much. I know he sent Tula that letter he wrote."

"Who and what letter?"

"Dawson. He told me he wrote out a confession letter about the night Bella died. He said he sent it to the only person he could trust. It had to be Tula."

"Steven, you mean your wife's sister? You're the one that killed her?"

"Yeah, and you're both gonna die, too, but we're going to have some fun first. I'll make sure it looks like I wasn't involved either. It'll look like a murder suicide when I'm done. You see, I've gotten very good at disposing the bodies over the years."

"Bodies?"

"There was more than just Bella. I buried one in the woods behind my house. Another I dumped in the bay. The prostitute I just threw in a dumpster in DC behind the motel where I killed her." He wrapped the rope around my torso one last time and made a tight knot.

He got inches from my face and turned the corners of his mouth into a malevolent smirk. "I'm going to fuck your little slut's brains out. And then bash her bitchy little face in before she dies. I like it when they cry and beg. You'll get to watch it happen. Yeah, that will be fun."

That's when I started to fight pointlessly against the ropes. I couldn't let Steven hurt her. When I kicked, I hit his shin. He returned the action with two hard punches. The first to the face. The second in the gut, knocking the wind out of me.

Chapter Fifty-Three

Tulip

WHEN I STOOD IN the darkness after Steven shot out the light, I had no clue what I was going to do next. I couldn't make an escape with the wooden skiff he brought us to The Stack on. There was no way I could get to the boat, board it, untie it, start the engine, and leave without him seeing and shooting me. Running for help had problems of its own, including the major one. I had no idea which direction to run. I had never seen the factory side of The Stack before, and in total darkness, there was nothing to guide me to safety.

I contemplated my options when I heard Steven scream, "Where the fuck did she go?!"

When we first got off the boat, I tried to make a mental inventory of where things were. North and east of The Stack from where the boat slip was, I remembered seeing three purse boats lined up along the water's edge.

I headed in the direction of the boats as quietly as possible. As I moved closer to the boats, I could hear Steven on the other side of the smokestack, circling it, searching for me.

"Tula? Where are you? I'm not gonna hurt you."

He was lying. I heard everything he said to Paul. His number one goal for me was pain and death.

Purse boats were workhorses and, like most hardworking equipment, needed constant maintenance. So, I wasn't shocked to see a variety of tools on the first boat I climbed upon. As I searched through the tools, I heard Steven call out for me over and over again. At first, he faked a friendly tone, but his anger and insanity seeped out more each time he called for me. He was closer each time as well.

"Tula? There's nowhere to run. I bet you're on one of these boats. I guess I'll have to check them all. When I find you, we're going to have fun."

I highly doubt that.

The darkness made it difficult as I frantically looked through the pile of tools in search of a weapon. As I clumsily looked, I found metal shears and used them to cut the zip tie, freeing my hands. I continued until at the bottom of the pile I found the perfect thing. A crowbar. It was hard, had a sharp claw at one end, and I could put more distance between Steven and me than I could with something like a screwdriver. I put one of those in the back pocket of my denim shorts as well. Just in case.

"Tula? Where the fuck are you?!"

His voice sounded deranged, desperate, and angry. He continued to mutter to himself, swearing profusely. That wasn't what concerned me, though. His voice sounded close. Too close. I felt the movement of the boat shaking as he climbed the ladder of the boat.

Now was the one chance I had to stop Steven. This had to work, but I did not know if I was strong enough to pull this off. I prayed I was because there were no other options. It was the moment of hurt or being hurt in a fight to survive.

I hid, crouched beside the spot where the ladder was attached to the boat, and waited. As I did, Paul screamed across the tiny peninsula where The Stack and the original factory building sat.

"Tulip, are you okay?! Answer me! Now!"

As much as I wanted to reassure him, I couldn't risk blowing the element of surprise.

When Steven's back was exposed as he leaned over the edge of the boat from the ladder to climb aboard, I stood and simultaneously lifted the crowbar over my head. I brought it down onto his back with all the strength I had. Steven screamed and stood on the top rung of the ladder outside the boat. I had failed, but he set up another chance for me when he stood upright on the ladder. I took the crowbar, positioned it like a golf club, and hit Steven under the chin like I was teeing off on the Mangrove Hole at the Key West Golf Club.

I watched as he fell backward, hitting his head on the hull of the boat next to us as he went down. I wasn't sure if he was dead or alive and really didn't want to get close enough to find out. As much as I wanted to get down the easy way, Steven was at the bottom of the ladder, and I didn't want to risk being attacked.

Paul yelled my name over and over again. However, my brain was too occupied with putting distance between me and Steven to respond. I looked over the starboard side of the purse boat but couldn't tell how far of a drop it was through the darkness, looked back at the ladder on the port side, and then jumped.

The ground was much farther than I anticipated. When I finally made contact with the ground, my ankle turned, and I heard cracking. The intense pain confirmed what I already knew. My left ankle was broken.

I stood. Trying not to apply weight to my left foot and failing. I needed to get to Paul, and there was only one way to do it. Crawl.

I was halfway to Paul when he yelled again. "Tulip Renée Yates, say something!"

"I'm coming to you, but it's going to take a while! I think I broke my ankle."

I moved as quickly as possible, and while I did, I thought a cloud that was covering the moon moved, giving me and Paul some much-needed light. A small smile formed on his lips when we finally saw each other. However, it wasn't the moon illuminating the space between me and Paul. It was a flashlight. So his smile only lasted a second before Paul yelled, "Steven!"

I pulled the screwdriver out of my pocket and rolled onto my back just as Steven tackled me, dropping his flashlight in the process. I reached up, shoved the screwdriver into his neck, pushed him off of me, and rolled him onto the ground. I lodged the tool into his throat just deep enough for blood to spurt out from his neck spraying everywhere. It only took ten seconds for Steven to lose consciousness.

I did nothing to try to stop the bleeding but sat and waited for the blood to stop spewing from his neck. It seemed like I watched for hours as the blood left Steven's body. However, it was less than two minutes before he stopped bleeding. I leaned over him long enough to pull the gun from his waistband, tuck it into the back of mine, and check his pulse. He did not have one.

Only then did I continue the painful crawl on the oyster shells to reach Paul. Without uttering a word, our lips pressed against each other before I untied the multiple knots binding him in his clothes.

After a few minutes, I muttered under my breath in frustration, "What the hell? Was Steven some kind of merchant marine?"

Once I had him free, we needed to get help, but there was so much I wanted to say. He grabbed my face by the chin and started talking first.

"Are you okay? How much of this blood is yours?"

"I don't think much of it is mine. Steven's blood ended up all over me," I said confidently.

Honestly, though, I had no idea. I was certain some of the shells that my face had been ground against by Steven's boot had drawn blood. He pulled up his T-shirt with his still bound hands and clumsily wiped the bulk of the blood from my face and neck.

We held each other tightly without uttering another sound before I felt his fingers holding my chin and tipping my head upward until my eyes locked with his. "Tulip, what letter was Steven talking about?"

"I don't know. But if Dawson sent it before he died, it would have gone to the house in Key West." It only took a few seconds for the light bulb moment to hit. "If he sent it to me, I know where it is. Callie sent me an envelope not long ago with mail in it. I never got around to opening it."

Chapter Fifty-Four

Paul

WE SAT INSIDE THE original factory building, which was now fantastic offices and conference rooms, waiting for help to arrive. Tulip and I felt bad about breaking a window to get inside but using one of their landline phones was the quickest way to call for help. While we waited for the police, Tulip wrote a note, and I left it on the desk in the office labeled Vice President after I used a pair of scissors I found in his assistant's desk to free myself from the zip tie. In the note, Tulip apologized for the damage and left her contact information, requesting they send her a bill for the repairs. She never received one.

The police arrived by land, parked in front of the building, and found us sitting in the lobby.

Detective Weston was the first officer on the scene closely followed by Dr. Floyd who volunteered with the rescue squad. They were listening to the police radio frequency when they heard our names and immediately headed to the fish factory. The detective was well-versed in our stories, so it took less time for us to explain the evening's events than I originally anticipated. Dr. Floyd quickly began to immobilize Tulip's ankle, and the possibility of a message from Dawson interested the detective.

"After you walk with me outside at the crime scene, I want to take you to Paul's and get a look at this letter."

"Not happening, Neil," the doctor said. "There's no way she's walking anywhere. She's got to go straight to the hospital for X-rays. The ankle is definitely broken. I just can't tell how severe the damage is yet."

"And I'm not letting her out of my sight," Paul added.

"Sir," Tulip said, looking nervously at the detective, "you do understand that I'm only speculating that the letter is in the envelope my roommate mailed me. I haven't actually seen it."

"I know. But your instincts have yet to be wrong on any of the events following Dawson's murder. You even had the presence of mind to email me a statement before you left Key West. So, for now, we'll assume the letter is there."

Two paramedics came in with a stretcher for Tulip. After they loaded her on, she rubbed her temple and winced in pain before looking up at Detective Weston. "How are we going to get that letter and keep these two happy?"

"Would either of you mind if I sent an officer to get the bag and meet us at the hospital?"

"Why the rush?" Paul asked.

"Because I don't want to have to charge Tula with anything. And if this letter says what Steven thinks it did, there's no reason to charge Tula with murder. It's cut and dry self-defense."

Chapter Fifty-Five

Paul

TULIP SAT IN THE hospital bed with her leg in a temporary cast. She would be going into surgery in a few hours to have her ankle repaired. I called The Colonel, who was on his way from Hampton and Lily was already in the waiting room. Once the police were done, she would join us.

Not long after we arrived, a nurse shooed everyone out. I wasn't happy about it, but Tulip convinced me it was fine and to go get myself some desperately needed coffee. When we were allowed back in, Tulip had been bathed, her hair washed free of blood, and wore a hospital gown. The nurse had gone to the pediatric ward to find one small enough to fit her. She was even beautiful in a hospital gown with panda bears printed all over it.

Tulip pulled a large envelope from the tote bag handed to her. She tore open the large brown envelope and poured smaller ones out of it. I watched as she picked out one and held it up. To the casual observer, there was nothing special about it. But we knew better. The address was written in Dawson's handwriting. Tulip stared at it, gently brushing the ink with her fingers. When she looked up, her eyes were filled with tears. If she blinked, they would fall. And they did.

Tulip looked at the detective. "Should I open it?"

The detective knew her better now than he did when Glenn died and saw how she questioned the obvious when stressed. "Yes, go ahead and read it, too."

She carefully opened the letter. She stared at it for a brief moment before she began to read aloud.

Tula,

By the time you get this letter, one of two things will have occurred. The first is the more likely. There's a good chance I will have been arrested along with Glenn and Steven. Many years ago, we were involved in the death of a seventeen-year-old girl. Her name was Bella. It was an accident, but we were all so scared we made a vow to never speak of it. And none of us have until now. I can't live with the guilt of the way we handled that night. I'm going to the police in the morning.

Once I've made a full confession, I think a bunch of things I've begun to suspect are going to come to the surface about Steven, and it won't be pretty. If you ever make your way back to Jett's Landing, check on Steven's wife, Peggy. She'll need the support. Bella was her sister.

The second possibility is that Steven will kill me to keep me quiet. I don't think he'd do that, but if I'm wrong, give this letter to the police in Jett's Landing. It will help them.

Paul will be the only partner of The Oyster Bar & Grill not caught up in this mess. His phone number is at the bottom of this page. He'll act like running the restaurant alone is no big deal, but he's going to need a friend. I know I'm asking a lot but be that friend to him. Check in with him. If he ever tells you his story, you'll understand. I would hate for him to relapse after all this time.

Tula, I'm sorry to lay all of this on you. I know people see you and think you have a charmed life, but I know better. You've been through the wringer and back again. You're the only person I trust to help me correct the wrongs of my messed-up life.

I love you cuz,

Dawson

"It makes sense now," I said.

"What makes sense?" Tulip asked me as Detective Weston listened intently to our conversation.

"'Find Tula. She'll know,'" Paul said. "He assumed you would have read the letter by the time I found the note."

The detective raised a brow as he stared at us. We had some explaining to do.

Chapter Fifty-Six

Tulip

"ARE YOU READY? We're going to be late."

Paul walked over to me and cupped my face in his hands. "No, babe, we won't. The doors won't open without us. I have the keys." He smiled before he kissed me gently over the faded scar on my cheek just under my left eye and then took my hand.

It and the surgical scars on my ankle were the only visible remnants of the night at The Stack. I still had the occasional nightmare, reliving what happened. When I did, Paul would hold me and gently wake me. He did everything gently with me these days.

"Let's go."

Paul helped me into the passenger's side of the truck, treating me like a fragile crystal candy dish. Once he was settled into the driver's side and backed out of the driveway, I watched as we rounded the corner and The Stack came into view. It was a short trip, and we were at the end of Jett's Landing in under a minute.

Paul and I could have walked, but there were three cases of liquor, four cases of champagne, and a large three-tiered cake with us. I looked around. I had been there hundreds of times in the last few months, but it seemed different. It wasn't just because people had gathered. It was more. I was home. George was roaming around town somewhere, enjoying the warm summer day, but I wasn't worried. He'd show up at the restaurant around noon, eat, lap down a ton of water, and then take a nap in the shade near the docks. We landscaped a shady area, especially for George, and he not only took full advantage of it but welcomed other four-legged friends as well.

It was just shy of a year since I drove into town for Dawson's funeral. I went back to the Keys in October and Paul went with me. It was only to pack things up, quit my job, and make arrangements to sell the house to my longtime roommate. When we returned to Jett's Landing just before the holidays, it was for good and there was no doubt in my mind it was the right decision.

Paul made his way to the front door of the new restaurant. We were opening a few weeks later than we originally hoped, and it worried me to no end. Paul spent many evenings assuring me that this was completely normal in the restaurant industry.

I followed the path to the door, and my palms began to sweat as I played with the band of diamonds on my left ring finger. It was the first time I wore it in public. For the last six months, everyone asked when we were getting married. Everyone, but my father. He already knew the answer. He and Paul's mom were the only witnesses when we wed at the beginning of March. Actually, I was shocked that my dad managed not to tell anyone. The man was terrible at keeping secrets where his daughters were concerned.

"Ladies and gentlemen," Paul began. "Tulip and I would like to thank y'all for coming out to help us celebrate the grand re-opening of The Oyster Bar & Grill."

I had given up on him ever calling me Tula again.

I looked around as Paul spoke. The entire town had come out for this event and then some. Paul's mother, brother, and family arrived last night. All six rooms at the Fisher House were being put to good use this week. My dad was in attendance along with all of my sisters, their spouses, and their children. I thought Lily might have already noticed my baby bump where my flat stomach once existed. It was getting harder and harder to hide, even under Paul's oversized T-shirts. Paul and I discovered just after Valentine's Day that the world we were building together would be growing in population.

I was still hesitant about marriage, but Paul was insistent that we marry the moment we discovered I was pregnant. He told me one night about a month after we wed that I knew we had done the right thing whether I realized it or not. How? He pointed out I had not said the phrase "This is a bad idea" since the day we said "I do."

I looked down at my ring again. I suddenly remembered a moment in time when Paul and I sat in the storeroom of the original restaurant talking of fake relationships and pretend babies. I smiled and happy tears welled up in my eyes.

There were many reasons I hadn't told my sisters about the marriage or the baby. I liked privacy in my relationships and knew I would be forever teased by my sisters for proving them right. I knew the fallout would be severe, but we couldn't keep this a secret much longer. Paul convinced me we should make all the announcements the day the restaurant reopened.

"Now many of you, okay, most of y'all, have asked when Tulip and I are going to get married. Well, you don't have to wait any longer. We already are and have been since the third of March." He held up his left hand, exposing a platinum band on his ring finger.

"So, tonight champagne and wedding cake are on the house. At least until we run out. And before you ask, yes, Tulip made the cake." The town recently discovered that my cakes were as good as my pies during a fundraising event for The Fishermen's Museum. Now they were going to be part of the new dessert menu. White cake with raspberry filling and lemon white chocolate cream cheese frosting seemed to be what everyone was talking about where I was concerned. I was certain that was about to change.

People in the crowd laughed, clapped, and my nieces and nephews bounced. Before the day was over, they would learn about my pregnancy, too.

Paul looked at me, and I smiled back at him. He was a happy man. I knew this because he told me daily. He had gotten the girl of his dreams, had a child on the way, and the restaurant that was his passion was again in one piece.

My novel was released in April and magically hit The New York Times bestseller list.

It rarely happened with first-time authors. The publisher eagerly awaited my next novel and my agent received a contract from a Hollywood producer who was interested in acquiring the movie rights. I was married to a man who adored me as no other man ever had, and I was expecting our daughter in late September. This was the life I had dreamt about for as long as I could remember.

As happy as I was, I was always happiest in Paul's arms. He walked over and leaned in from behind me, held me tightly, and whispered "I love you" as he kissed my neck. He rubbed my belly after smoothing out my shirt, making it obvious how pregnant I truly was.

When he did, I heard all four of my sisters gasp. That's when I relaxed and smiled. I didn't realize how nervous I was about sharing our news until that moment. It was then that I leaned my head back and whispered in his ear.

"I love you, too, but it's time to open The Oyster."

The End

Acknowledgments

As always, there are so many people I want to thank, and with each novel, the list gets longer. I'll begin with Charles and Olivia Williams, the owners of The Crazy Crab Restaurant in Reedville, Virginia. Years ago, when this book was only a seed of an idea, Charles was kind enough to arrange a before-hours tour of the entire restaurant. It helped in the formation of The Oyster Bar & Grill restaurant.

The Stack, a significant landmark within the story, is an actual monument on the grounds of the Omega Protein Headquarters and Processing Plant. Montgomery Deihl, CEO of Ocean Harvesters, and my uncle, Fred Rice, were kind enough to arrange access for me to visit The Stack after I commented on how I wished I get a closer look. Be careful what you wish for!

Omega Protein not only allowed me to explore The Stack from the fish factory side of the fence but connected me with Taylor Deihl, their marketing manager. She answered all of my crazy emails, provided me with plenty of time to explore The Stack's grounds, and gave me a fantastic tour of the factory. This field trip inspired me to look at the "finished" manuscript and ended with a complete re-write of the novel.

In addition, to the research contributors for this novel, there is also my reading team, whom I must thank as their feedback constantly improves my writing. First, is my alpha reader, novel therapist (If you know, you know.), and dear friend, Stefanie Lewis. You are the best when it comes to asking me, "How would your character feel?" And then there are my beta readers, Dezi Webler, Jen Laning, and Kathy Hawkins. I don't know how you do it, but you always see what is missing in the story. And finally, my editor, Samantha Pico of Miss Eloquent Edits. Thank you for turning my words into beautiful prose.

Also by Beth Sorensen

The Thomas Hall Series

Crush at Thomas Hall – Book One
Divorcing a Dead Man – Book Two
Waiting for Time to Tell – Book Three